Flanigan's Hotel

Christel Weingart worked for more than thirty years as a self-employed crafts woman in England, the South of France and Germany. Born in East Friesia, she loves the stories of that part of Germany, being one of a few people who speaks and writes in "Plattdeutsch" (Low German, one of the reconnised endangered languages in the world). She has written and published several short stories as well as novels in german and worked as a translator for Radio and Film. Since her retirement she lives and works near Berlin concentrating on novels and theatre plays.

CHRISTEL WEINGART

Flanigan's Hotel

From East Friesia to Newfoundland

Novel

Bibliographical Information of the Deutsche Nationalbibliothek

This publication is listed in the Deutsche Nationalbibliographie of the Deutsche Nationalbibliothek; detailed bibliographical information can be accessed under http: //dnb.d-nb.de

Flanigan's Hotel – From East Friesia to Newfoundland
Historic Novel by Christel Weingart
© 2023 Christel Weingart – All rights reserved by the author.
Translation: Christel Weingart
Editor/Lektor: Annette Morris
Cover Illustration: Grit Marrot
Original Title: Flanigans Hotel – Von Ostfriesland in die Neue Welt, published June 2022 by Criminal-kick-Verlag, Rhauderfehn, Germany
Printing, Production and Layout: BoD – Books on Demand, Norderstedt
ISBN: 978-3-7578-6470-5

Flanigan's Hotel – The Story

In the year 1908 four families from East Frisia, which lies on the coast of northern Germany and close to the Dutch border, decide to emigrate to North America. They find a steam freighter in the harbour of Emden which takes them on board. After a rough crossing through the North Sea and a mysterious nightly stop somewhere along the Irish coast, the group, after crossing the Atlantic, arrives tired and weak one night at a dimly lit harbour and are made to disembark by order of the captain. They soon realise that they have not been dropped in the land of their dreams – America. A great adventure with unexpected ups and downs lies ahead of them.

All characters and actions in this book are fictitious. Resemblance to any real persons – living or deceased – is purely coincidental.

List of persons as they appear in the book:

East Friesia:

Viktoria Brendel	Spinster from Hannover
Dr. Brendel	Father of Viktoria, deceased
Elisabeth Reiners	Cousin of Viktoria
Uda Reiners	Daughter, 10 years old
Feemke Reiners	Daughter, 8 years old
Enno Reiners	Son, 4 years old
Harm Reiners	Husband, Farmer
Dirtje Bontjes	Maid of Reiners Family
Eske Bontjes	Mother
Johannes Bontjes	Brother
Ocko Bontjes	Brother, horse expert
Advocat Meyerdirks	Solicitor of Reiners Family
Jan Reiners	Brother of Harm, Groningerland
Hendrike Reiners	Wife of Jan
Wim Redenius	Captain of Freighter "Concordia"
Jan Janssen	Ship yard worker from Emden
Gerti Janssen	Wife
Emmi Janssen	Daughter, 14 years old
Hinnerk Frerichs	Fisher from Greetsiel
Sina Frerichs	Wife

Hajo Lammers	Boat builder from Timmel
Thalea Lammers	Wife
Freerk Lammers	Son, 10 years old

Newfoundland:

Edan Flanigan	Hotel Owner in St. Johns
Jim Flanigan	Husband
Pierre Leclerc	Police Constable
Dr. James Waldron	Doctor in Portgual Cove and Bell Island
Mabel	Maid on Bell Island
Patrick O'Leary	Fabric shop owner
Alec Morrison	Geologist on Bell Island
Mister O'Sullivan	Sweet shop owner
Jeremia Appleby	Sewing machine representative
Albertus Meiners	Prisoner in Halifax

*Sometimes we just
have to follow
our dreams.*

Part 1

East Frisia

Chapter 1

The old man coughed nervously and stepped from one leg to the other.

"Excuse me, Miss Brendel. We are ready. Everything is packed and the carriage is waiting. You'll have to go now otherwise you'll miss the train. Time to say good-bye."

Viktoria turned and looked at the old man. He had been part of her life since childhood. She would dearly miss him. "Oh Jakob, only one more moment, please. I want to go through the empty house one more time to say good-bye to the place. I won't be long. Please go ahead."

Viktoria saw him shrug his shoulders and turn. As she walked from room to room, looking at the walls with the faded wallpapers and the ceilings with decorative plaster work, she felt sadness and relief at the same time. Suddenly she turned back to the entrance. This was already history. The house was sold. This chapter of her life here in Hannover was definitely over. She promised herself not to fret and look to the future instead. This would make life easier. She stepped outside into a bright, spring morning and pulled the door closed firmly. Four steps led down to the garden and gravelled drive.

Jakob Steinbach stood by the carriage and opened the door as she approached. She hated good-byes, especially today when she parted forever and would never see this faithful servant of her father again. How long had he been part of her household? She couldn't remember. He always had been there when he was needed. She took his wrinkled hands into hers and gave them a gentle squeeze.

"Thank you for everything. Thank you so much for all your help during the last weeks and months. I wish you all the best for your retirement. You more than deserve a rest now. As soon as I arrive I will write to you. We will stay in touch."

She put her arms around the little man so suddenly that he – surprised by the gesture – tried to step back in shock.

"God bless you, Miss." His voice broke. He turned away in order to hide his tears.

Viktoria climbed into the horse-drawn carriage and Jakob gave the order to start.

As the carriage reached the first bend in the street she took a last look back at the house. It stood there, proud, tall and empty. Along the wrought iron fence she saw the forsythia in the height of their bloom. She had always loved the garden, and Spring was a special time for her. Memories came up. Memories of the day when she and her father had planted a few sprigs along this very fence. She must have been seven or eight. The forsythia had been standing in a vase on the sideboard, amongst Viktoria's hand-painted Easter eggs. As Easter was over the maid came to dispose of the twigs, but when Viktoria saw the fine little white roots at the end of each twig, she begged her father to plant them in the garden. He had smiled at her. "Well, let´s go then. We will see if they will grow into big, strong bushes, my petal." He'd smiled at her. Typical dad, he could not deny a wish like that. And as she grew into a teenager and then adulthood the twigs grew into big bushes. Every springtime passing pedestrians stopped in admiration and awe of the yellow splendour.

As the carriage reached the main boulevard leading to the railway station Viktoria leaned back into her seat and closed her eyes. What time would she arrive at the town of Emden? Would her cousin Elisabeth come to meet her? Or would Elisabeth's husband be waiting? She could hardly remember Harm Reiners, the rich farmer of the Polder[1] area. Would she be able to recognise him after all these years? She remembered him as a tall blond man with incredibly blue eyes. When Elisabeth introduced him days before the wedding Viktoria was quite taken with him. The couple had visited her in Hannover. But that was years ago. Elisabeth had since given birth to three children and the only contact between the cousins had been the exchange of occasional letters. Now she was on her way to help her family. A new challenge, she hoped. Since her father's death she'd needed a new purpose in life. She was already thirty, an old spinster. She could have looked for a job as a nanny but decided against it. Looking after other people's children didn't seem right when she knew that her cousin could do with some help because of her fragile constitution. Her

---

1   Polder – farmland re-gained from the sea, fertile land. The word comes from the Dutch language.

family needed her and it was her duty to comply. She shivered in anticipation.

The carriage had to stop a few times on the way due to heavy traffic but they reached the station just in time for her train. She quickly paid the coachman, grabbed her two heavy, leather bags and walked briskly through the entrance hall. She had to hurry if she wanted to catch her train. With ticket and bag in her right hand she approached the controller at the barrier. As she finally entered the second class railway carriage she fell exhausted into an empty seat by the window.

Chapter 2

East Frisia, Spring 1908

After changing trains at Bremen, Oldenburg and Leer, the train was just leaving for the last stretch of her journey to Emden. Suddenly anxiety crept up on her. What was she doing here? She looked through the dirty windows of her compartment, outside a bleak and flat landscape went by. Nothing but endless meadows, here and there a group of black and white cows grazing in the light of a giant, open sky. In the far distance red roofs of farmhouses surrounded by bushes and tall, bare trees. Nothing else for miles. As they were coming closer to the town of Emden she spotted a vivid green strip on the horizon to the left. "This must be the dyke of the river Ems" she thought. From Elisabeth´s last letter she knew that her destination was coming closer. Emden wouldn't be far now.

The train was running late as it reached Emden station. She disembarked stiffly and walked along the platform, passing a few farmers' families with chickens in cages and children. Viktoria had searched for a known face as she got off the train, but neither here nor anywhere else did she see one. So she walked towards the barrier, the controller took her ticket, stared at it for a moment and deposited the little brown card in this leather book. Then he opened the barrier so that she could go through into the main entrance hall. As she left this rather dingy place she was blinded by the light outside. It took a moment for her eyes to adjust. She spotted a bench, sat down, her bags close to her body, and waited. Somebody would come to fetch her she said to herself.

Not far from her stood two carriages waiting for paying passengers. One of the coachmen looked at her and gave her an encouraging smile, revealing his rotten, brown teeth. She shuddered and turned away in disgust.

Viktoria only noticed the young lad the moment he stood right in front of her. Full of uncertainty he asked her if she was the visitor to the Reiner´s farm. He had been sent to fetch her.

She stood up with great relief and stretched her hand out to greet him. But he ignored it, grabbed the two bags and walked towards an open-framed carriage drawn by a huge, black horse. With a brisk movement he threw the bags onto the luggage rack and indicated for Viktoria to climb up into the seat. She scrambled up and took the seat next to him. Just at this moment her skirt was lifted by a gust of wind, exposing her legs, showing her black stockings. The coachmen nearby whistled and cheered so that she blushed with embarrassment, wishing she could leave a bit faster, but the black horse was in no hurry.

After a one hour journey at leisurely pace, coming through the wide ,open landscape of the Krummhoern[2] with its Warfen-Villages[3] and massive red-brick

---

2   Krummhoern – A large part in the west of East Frisia,, formerly part of the North sea, reclaimed by the Frisians after the year 800 AD. The dykes directly on the coast were called sea dykes, the old ones – later replaced due to the gain of more land – were called summer dykes. Those areas were then named summer polder.
3   Warfendoerfer (Wharfs) In order to save themselves from regular flooding they started to build man-made hills for their

churches, they finally reached their destination – a huge brick-built farmhouse, exclusively typical to this part of the coast. The Gulfhof[4] had a two-storey living quarters with sash windows and a grand double entrance door. As they came closer she noticed a maid coming out of a side door, carrying a milk churn in each hand which she stood upside down onto a wooden shelf along the wall. The largest part of the building was the attached high barn containing the stables for the horses, pigs and cattle as well as a huge hay loft and a threshing floor. The barn building had an access on the side as well on the back so that carriages could drive through to unload inside.

As they arrived at the farmhouse two girls came running out. Viktoria had never met them in person but knew they must be ten year old Uda and eight year old Feemke. Both seemed very excited to see her and as they stood in front of her, out of breath, they curtsied, as well educated young ladies would be expected to do. Viktoria laughed and took them into her arms. But where was their little brother, the four year old Enno? She asked the girls about him but they only shrugged their shoulders.

"Aunt Viktoria, Aunt Viktoria! Come in! Let´s go to see

---

houses and farms. In the 12th century they built churches with big square towers which gave them not only safety in case of flooding, but also in case of war.

4   Gulfhof – this type of traditional farm building appeared in the 18th century all along the coast of West Frisia (Netherlands) and East Frisia to demonstrate the incredible wealth of the farmers there. The land – formerly under the sea – was a rich clay soil and ideal for the growing of potatoes, cabbage and roots which were sold to the surrounding towns.

mother. She is ill in bed again. She is waiting for you." Feemke took Viktorias hand and pulled her towards the front door. Viktoria turned around quickly to the carriage, looking for her luggage and she saw him. He stood in the huge open barn door, straw in his hair and on his clothes, buttoning up his corduroy trousers. His puffy face was red and sweaty and as he looked at her now there was a vile grin on his face. Full of disgust she turned away, quickly entering the house. It was Harm Reiners, Elisabeth´s husband. He had aged and grown fat. But what really disturbed her was the way he had looked at her. There had been something evil in his blue eyes. It frightened her.

Slightly upset after this brief encounter, she followed the girls upstairs to the couple's bedroom. Viktoria stood in shock in the open doorway when she saw Elisabeth. Was this her cousin? Elisabeth looked old and pale amongst all the bulky feather cushions and quilt and she seemed so frail.

"Aunt Viktoria is here!" both girls shouted at the same time. "Mother, Aunt Viktoria has really come! Look!"

Elisabeth opened her eyes and stretched her hand out to her visitor. Viktoria took it and bent down to kiss her cousin's forehead. It was cold as ice but damp. Then a sobbing noise came from the bed as Elisabeth tried to sit up. "I never thought this would ever happen, you are really here. Now everything will be alright, all will turn for the better." With those words she sunk back onto her pillows. Viktoria was shocked. The woman in bed was deathly pale and her formerly blond hair had turned grey and dull. It was hard to believe that this was the same person, so young, full of life and laughing who had come to visit her in Hannover only eleven years ago. Viktoria remembered being a little bit jealous at that time, her cousin had met an attractive, rich, young farmer and seemed to be happy and in love. What had happened since? Her first thought was that here lies a very unhappy woman who takes refuge in illness. For some unknown reason Viktoria was more than convinced of that.

Then she told the family about her journey and the girls listened in awe. They had never seen a train. Suddenly the bedroom door opened and a young maid appeared with a tray, serving tea. Viktoria gave a quick glance in her direction and continued to speak. She was not much older than perhaps fourteen, small and dainty, her red hair hidden under a bonnet, she didn't look at anybody, avoiding eye contact. A tray was placed on the marble top of the bedside table next to Elisabeth. The girl was about to leave when Elisabeth called her back.

"Dirtje, come here my dear", she whispered. Dirtje came closer again. Now Viktoria took a closer look. The girl's face was swollen and there were bits of straw clinging to her bonnet and skirt. The girl had obviously been crying. Elisabeth tried to sit up again and reached her hand towards the maid but she again took a step back and was about to leave. "Dirtje, come here, let me have a look at you." This time Elisabeth´s voice was stronger. The girl came closer again und stood by the bedside. Elisabeth took Dirtje´s little hand into hers and looked at her. "I am so sorry. So very sorry to lie here and not being able to help you. One day he will get his punishment and go to hell. God will give justice, this I promise you. With that she sunk once more onto her pillows and closed her eyes. A deep groan came from her chest. Dirtje pulled her hand back and fled crying from the room. Viktoria was horrified. The girls looked silently down to their shoes, then, meaningfully, at Viktoria.

Chapter 3

Viktoria stood at the rails on the deck of a large ship and looked out at the sea. The sun had just reached the horizon where it would disappear in shades of red and orange. Viktoria waited for this moment. But suddenly the sun was gone and the sea dark. Out of the water her cousin, Elisabeth, rose up. She grew and grew and eventually filled the whole sky. Viktoria was terrified. Elisabeth had seaweed hanging around her head instead of hair. Her eyes seemed huge and black. She lifted her right hand and spoke with a loud and haunting voice:

"I curse you, Polder farmer. Go to hell." Then Elisabeth sunk back into the dark waters. A ship's bell started to ring. "Man over board, man over board", she tried to scream but her voice was hardly there. Nobody heard her and nobody came to her cousin's rescue. Full of panic, she paced up and down the deck. Somebody had to help her. But nobody was in sight. The ship's bell became louder and louder.

The door of her bedroom was opened and Uda stepped towards the bed and watched her aunt who obviously had had a bad dream. The girl knew all about bad dreams and looked at Viktoria in pity.

"Aunt Victoria, please wake up. The bell is ringing for supper. It's time to eat. Please get up and come with me."

Viktoria left the land of dreams, more like nightmares, and sat up. It took her a moment to recognise the girl. It all was just a bad dream. Realising this, she got up quickly and tidied her hair, then she searched for her boots and followed Uda.

Uda took her down into the servants' kitchen which was warm and cosy. The large white cooking stove sent a smell of a roast in her direction. Viktoria suddenly realised how hungry she was. She looked at the long wooden table in the middle of the room. No table cloth. Only two huge frying pans were placed at the centre. Around the table were the four farmhands and three maids, one of them being Dirtje who looked away as she approached. She greeted the young lad that had fetched her from the station but he also looked away, inspecting the table top closely. The cook, a sturdy figure in her fifties with a chubby red face, brought a loaf of bread to the table. "Tuck in", she announced and took her place at the head of the table. Viktoria was uncertain where she would eat. Here? At this table? Where was the farmer and where were the children? The cook looked in her direction and pointed to an empty stool at the far end of the table. "This is going to be your place from now on", she commanded. Uda's face had turned red and she fled the scene."They are eating with their father in the dining room." the cook explained with a grin. "You are staying with us now you are working here." The others around the table giggled. So that's it. This was unexpected for Viktoria. She wasn't sure whether to laugh or cry. Time would tell, but perhaps everything was a mistake and as soon as Harm Reiners appeared she would demand an explanation. But he never came that evening.

She watched the others eat and did what they did. She took her fork, dipped it into the huge frying pan and tried to spear a little round potato, moving it through a thick gravy and back to her mouth. The others watched her and the maids started to giggle. The potato made it half way across the table, then fell off and landed on the wooden table. The giggle increased, even on the other side of the table. Viktoria tried to catch the potato again but with no luck. So she decided on using her fingers and it worked. Relief everywhere. The cook nodded approvingly. Victoria´s fingers were meanwhile full of greasy, stodgy gravy, she could have done with a napkin but they were no-where to be found. The smacking and burping from the men nearly made her lose her appetite. But she carried on, potato after potato. She was hungry and didn´t want to leave her share of the food to the others. Everybody here had obviously more practice in this kind of eating and soon both pans were empty except for the stodgy gravy. This was wiped up with the slice of bread. Viktoria had to admit that the gravy was tasty, containing bacon cubes, onion and milk. How little did she know that soon she would despise this meal since it came every second day on the table. The others never complained because it filled their stomachs. The staff at this farm were lucky in comparison to others working in the area. At least they went to bed with a full stomach. They knew they should be thankful. Nevertheless, after a few days Viktoria would demand plates for everyone. A bit of culture wouldn´t do any harm she thought.

After supper she decided to search the children to say good night. But they were not be found, nor their father. So she wandered along the hallway, listening carefully at all doors she was passing, hoping to hear the girls somewhere. As she passed the door which she had entered to see Elisabeth earlier that day she heard the rhythmical squeak of a bed and the loud and lustful groan of a man. She blushed and fled to her room. The moment she closed the door behind her she threw up – straight into the wicker basket which was standing next to her. Only then Viktoria realised that this was not the right kind of vessel. The mess ran through the openings and spread over the wooden floor boards. But she couldn´t be bothered and threw herself onto the bed, pulling the cover over her head, not even undressing and crying her eyes out.

Through her tears she sank down into the land of dreams, to a place that seemed strangely familiar. She stood on deck of a ship looking at the sunset and a horrible feeling crept up on her. She tried to remember and looked, full of panic, out at the sea...

Chapter 4

Johannes Bontjes stretched out his limbs as he lay in the midday sun. He was lying on a dry patch of grass, surrounded by flowering heather, day-dreaming. The crickets sang, as did a blackbird perched nearby in the little birch tree. Here, in the shallow dip of the high-moor, he was sheltered from the cold sea wind.

"Back to work you lazy loafer!" It was his father calling. He stood at the edge of the moor leaning on the handle of his wide spade. It was Sunday and they had worked since the early morning cutting peat. The high-moor had been growing over thousands of years, heavy and saturated by the dark brown waters. Eske Bontjes piled up the brick-like pieces onto the wooden wheelbarrow and brought the peat to a flat area nearby. It was the job of the older children to pile them up, building little roundish towers with gaps in between the pieces so that the wind could blow through and dry them. The job of the smaller children was to turn each piece of turf so that every side would be dried by the sun and wind. By that time the pieces had already lost most of their weight. Behind their ramshackle houses built of clay and thatched with straw or if people were really poor, with turf, nearly every inhabitant of the moors owned a narrow stretch of land. Cutting the peat ensured the poor people would have something to heat and cook with and if they were lucky, and the summer weather good, they could produce a little surplus and sell it.

Johannes stood up and stretched his limbs. His

bones ached and he could hardly stand upright anymore. The last eight Sundays he had been helping his parents cut the peat which was very hard work. He watched his mother, a thin but tough woman, as she pushed the loaded wheelbarrow to the drying place. Her body had the colour of the peat – dark brown and leathery. Every summer was like that. In winter she looked pale and tired. He was the eldest of ten children who all lived – apart from his sister Dirtje, who worked on a farm – with his parents in the little hut on the edge of the moor. Dirtje had gone away two years ago and he thought how lucky she had been to find a job as a maid in a wealthy household. He and the family had only seen her once since she had started work though. She was nearly an adult now and he was incredibly proud of her making her own life. The Polder farmer Harm Reiners came every year at the end of summer to buy some turf from Johannes's family and pay Dirtje's wages to their parents. It was a longstanding tradition. The Bontjes family had supplied the Reiners family for generations and his parents were proud that they could continue to do so, and to have such a long-lasting customer. It was the only money that came in and they could buy things which the company-house did not offer. The company owned all the large turf cutting sites, the canals and boats, the machines and the rails and tubs needed for transport. The people working for them were not paid in money but received vouchers which they could use to buy everyday things at the company-owned stores at expensive prices. Everybody had been complaining about it – to no avail. The vouchers didn´t feed the large families any longer. So most people tried to get some other income and only bought necessary food, shoes, fabric and fodder for the animals at the company store. Some were lucky enough to keep a goat or a pig and some chickens. Then they had some milk, some eggs and, at Christmas perhaps, a boiled chicken in the pot.

Johannes took over from his father. The old man walked with a bent back to his wife and asked for a bit of bread and water.

"Take some of the fatty bacon, dear, you have to stay strong," his wife ordered. But he refused, wanting to leave the meat for Johannes and the other children. They needed the fat more in order to get some protection from tuberculosis – an illness quite common in this part of the world. He sat down to take a little rest.

"We have to cut another three rows today", he murmured, "Reiners will be here next Thursday to collect the first load. I just hope he brings Dirtje with him this time. She must have grown a bit since we saw her last." His wife snorted and gave some answer only to be off again pushing the empty wheelbarrow back over to the cutting pit. She managed twelve bricks of peat each time, more were too heavy for a woman. Strong men could manage double. But this was usually a woman's work, at least in this family. What other families did was of no interest. Everybody was working for themselves, but only in their spare time; in the evenings and on Sundays. The main work was done for the company which owned all the large moors between Norden, Aurich and Emden and made a fortune by exploiting the workers. Families like the Bontjes were merely hired labourers.

Nevertheless – Johannes loved his job at the moor company. Two years before he had been promoted unexpectedly, suddenly put in charge of the little train which transported the harvested peat to the works. Since then his work had been easier. It was thanks to his colleague Hein Ennenga. Hein had been the driver for many years, knew how to keep the rails in order and service the junctions, and he was the foreman's favourite because he was a musician. The foreman – a red-haired guy who loved his Schnapps (alcohol made from potatoes) loved to hear Hein playing his accordion. Hein and Johannes had worked together for a number of years and Johannes had asked many questions about the train. Soon he knew everything there was to know. So on the day Hein dropped dead on one of his tours, they collected his body and Johannes just took over his job and worked until the end of the shift. Nobody mentioned this change, it was only when he finished working that the foreman patted his shoulder and commented: "Well done. You've got a new job. Now you will have to learn how to make music. Otherwise we will have to look for somebody else." At the end of the week he received his pay rise. But the price of beer had just gone up too. Nothing was really gained.

Whilst Johannes and his older brothers worked with their parents at the peat bog, the younger kids had their own fun around the house. The Bontjes children chased the chickens, set traps for rabbits and threw mud at each other. They were a noisy lot. Even when the weather was bad the hut was too small for all of them at once. Ten children was normal in many families. As the evening approached mother would move the table and stools aside and the complete floor would be covered with hessian sacks to sleep on. In the morning they were gathered up and stuffed into their parents' two cupboard-like beds on one of the walls. They were closed up during the day with wooden doors. Then the long, rough made bench, table and stools were placed in the middle again. But not all ten children could sit to eat at the same time. Some sat on the floor or even outside when the weather allowed it.

The great pride of the household was a cooking stove. Most poor people used an open fire to heat and cook. But Eske had been given this stove as a wedding present by her parents. And she looked after it. Polishing the top was a regular Saturday job. Sometimes, when the children tried to steal a spoonful during cooking and a drop of food landed on the shiny surface, she would get cross. The children would run outside laughing and she would go after them with a broom shouting "Devil's brood" and she would laugh as well. The children ran onto the moor. Eske felt happy, ten children and all were healthy and alive. She should be more than grateful. But these wretched men! Every year another child. One should tie a knot in their thingy. At this thought she grinned and went back to the stove. That was her life. They were poor but cheerful, sometimes a bit too cheerful. And nine months later the result was to be seen and heard. Then they told the children: Where there are nine there's room for ten." And everybody smiled.

Chapter 5

Straight away after supper, Dirtje went up to her little chamber above the cow shed. She had to prepare for her trip tomorrow. The thought of seeing her parents again excited her. After all, she hadn't seen her parents since last autumn. And her visit at Christmas had been cancelled at the last minute because the maid Elsa had been taken ill. Instead of seeing her family she helped the cook prepare the elaborate meal for the farmer's family and she even had to serve at the table. Tomorrow she would join Harm Reiners and Miss Brendel when they collected the first load of peat. Dirtje was more than glad that she would not be alone with the farmer on this trip. He would not dare to touch her on the way to her parents, but who knows? Perhaps on the way back? You'll never know with him, she thought.

Since Viktoria had arrived at the farm some things had changed for the better. The lady of the house seemed more cheerful and got out of bed more often and even the children looked happier. Now there was laughter in the house. And the cook was content because Viktoria praised her cooking. This encouraged the woman to offer a whole variety of new meals to put on the table and Viktoria discovered a lot more local dishes that she really liked. Also, there were now plates for everybody and real cutlery. At first the maids and workmen thought it strange but soon they adapted and after a few days it had become normality. Even the bad behaviour during meals had ceased.

They didn´t dare to misbehave in the company of a lady.

Viktoria still didn´t know her position in this household. She didn´t seem to be part of the family and at the same time she wasn´t a member of the staff. But everybody knew she was the cousin of the lady of the house. It was a strange situation for all. But in the end she didn´t really care. Most important was that she would attend to the children. "I am here for the children and everybody else that needs me. Only this matters." she kept saying to herself.

Dirtje watched Viktoria secretly observing Harm Reiners. The result was that he lost interest in her and she felt more at ease when he was around. Whenever Viktoria was nearby, he seemed to feel that he had to behave.

Dirtje sat down on her plain wooden bed with the straw mattress. Then she searched around and pulled a paper bag from under the straw. It contained all her treasures: a small ornamental tortoiseshell comb, given to her by her mother years ago, a hymn book which she would take to church – if she ever had the time to go. In church she would pretend to read from it when she sang, but her reading skills were not sufficient for complicated words like that. She knew most of the hymns anyway. She just pretended to read. And then she pulled out a little curl of blond hair. She smiled. It belonged to Jan, the boy who kissed her when she was ten. Afterwards she had taken a pair of scissors and cut off a little lock of his hair as a treasure. He had laughed but his mother wasn't amused when he returned home and he'd got a good hiding. She hadn´t seen him for a few years but knew from his sister – who also worked at a farm in her area – that he now lived on the island of Norderney working as a coachman, fetching tourists from the boat and taking them to their accommodation. Those summer guests apparently gave him huge tips because he was a friendly and good looking chap. His sister had told Dirtje that some weeks he had more tip money than wages. And he was saving all the extra money for his future. Dirtje wondered what this future might be and if she would be part of it.

At the very bottom of the paper bag was her latest treasure: a large button made of seashell which she had found on the road to Norden. It just lay there, glistening in the sun. She had never seen such a button before and decided that she would put it on her smock for tomorrow. She would sew it right in the middle of the bodice front so everybody could see it. Quickly she got the little sewing kit out that her mother had given her when she had left home and fixed the button onto the fabric. She hoped her mother would like the button as much as she did.

After she put her remaining treasures back into the paper bag she went downstairs to fetch fresh water from the well. Upstairs she washed her body and her hair using a piece of soap which Viktoria had given her as a present shortly after she had arrived at the farm. Dirtje loved the scent of it – violet. From Hannover! The other maids, with whom she shared the chamber, were allowed to use the soap as well but only on Sundays. The girls had been much more friendly towards Dirtje lately and her fear of the maids had vanished. Quite often they provided her with an extra chunk of bread now from the kitchen. They knew Dirtje was always hungry. When she finished washing and dressing she looked at the smock again. The shiny button made it very special. Now she was looking forward to her trip.

Viktoria also prepared for her daytrip. She too washed her long hair and gave it a good brush until the hair was dry. Then she decided on a new hair style. Instead of putting her hair up using combs and pins she just bound it together in the neck and knotted a blue scarf around it. This was daring but for a trip to the moor it seemed practical. She admired her reflection in the little silver-framed hand mirror which her father had presented to her on her twenty-first birthday.

Harm Reiners used the early evening to check the spokes and wheels of the open framed carriage, then he went to the pair of horses he would need the next day, checking their hooves and bridles. Everything seemed alright. Satisfied, he looked around the stable, got his pipe out and sat down on the corn box to have a quiet smoke. Tomorrow he would travel with two women. A tempting thought. Perhaps on the way back he would stop and have a bit of fun with one of them. He should try it with the old spinster. He imagined how she would react, scream and fight. But this normally turned him on. He hoped she hadn´t dried up too much. The maid in comparison had become boring the moment she had stopped trying to fend him off. Since Viktoria had arrived at the farm he had watched her and her broad and flat behind had been part of his dreams at night. He would show this snooty and arrogant woman who the boss was.

At the same time Elisabeth curled up in her bed. She thought about her time as a young girl, spending her vacations at her uncle's house in Hannover, where he was a well-respected Doctor. He had been so friendly and kind to her and she saw him as a kind of father figure since her own father had suddenly died. She had only been ten at the time. Officially he had died as a result of a tragic hunting accident but Elisabeth knew better. The kitchen staff had talked about it secretly. He had committed suicide after the lodge he belonged to had suggested to him to end his life. Supposedly there was money missing. A lot of money. But what seemed worse – he had lost his honour. Her mother never recovered from the shock and shame and had drowned at the age of thirty two. Elisabeth´s life had never been the same since. The contact with her uncle and especially with Viktoria had helped her through the dark times as the girls kept writing to each other. Letters full of dreams and teenage matters. When Elisabeth was about sixteen she even thought that she had fallen in love with her cousin. She told Viktoria and her cousin reacted with laughter. Soon both forgot about this again. But now that Viktoria was part of her daily life again she sought her company whenever possible. They sat in the evening in the parlour together, talking about literature, the theatre and concerts. Elisabeth couldn´t hear enough of all this, realising how much she had missed out on. Why had Viktoria given all this up in order to live here? Surely, because she secretly still loved her. This thought comforted her every minute and made life with her husband – at least for the moment – more bearable.

Chapter 6

Viktoria woke up early feeling full of energy and got out of bed. She looked out of the window. It would be another hot day judging by the blue sky. She was full of anticipation. A trip to the moorlands sounded interesting. Downstairs in the kitchen the cook had prepared the usual breakfast – porridge. The farmhands had already eaten and were on their way to the stables. Cows had to be milked, the pigs and chickens to be fed. They fetched the horses to harness them.

Viktoria sat down to eat. A moment later she was joined by Dirtje. She had to smile when she saw the young girl with her smock and the button on it. The cook also noticed the button and shook her head at the foolishness of the maid.

"How long will we take to get to the moorland?" Viktoria asked. Dirtje didn´t have to think. "About an hour, depending which way the farmer is taking. He can go via Georgsheil or Marienhafe." Viktoria had never heard these names before, she found them foreign. "And where do your parents live?" Dirtje put up her chin and smiled. "Rechtsupweg", she answered dryly. "Yes, that is the street but I have asked for the village", corrected Viktoria. Now Dirtje burst out laughing. She knew nobody ever believed that a village was named like that. "Rechtsupweg is the name of the village!" Now she really started to laugh. Those people from town were sometimes a bit slow.

Viktoria felt a bit stupid. She finished her breakfast in silence and then got up to fetch her bag and straw hat from upstairs. She certainly would need a hat today.

Meanwhile the cook had packed a lunch basket for them. A cold leg of ham and a beer for the boss, in addition to a loaf of bread as well as cheese and a bottle of watered- down red currant juice for the women. Everything was wrapped in a teacloth together with three stoneware mugs and a knife. She checked again to make sure nothing was missing. Last time she had forgotten the knife and the farmer had been very angry and in the evening she had suffered because of it. Never again! She knew how violent his reactions could be. She didn´t want to take any risks. How could his fine wife put up with him? Or the children? She felt pity for the girls. They were non-existent to him. Often he complained that women were useless to him, couldn´t manage a farm. Only his son Enno received his attention. Which also meant that he spoiled him. That boy listened to nobody but his father. He was a real little devil already. The cook shuddered to think what would become of a child like that. Then she took the lunch basket and placed it in the carriage. The horses were already harnessed and ready for the trip.

Harm Reiners came outside, in a jovial mood as he looked around. Viktoria stood ready to leave. She looked attractive in her blue dress and the straw hat. Years ago his wife had worn dresses like that, but since she'd lived here on the farm she wore dark clothes and her hair looked unkempt. And her pinched face...it made him angry. She was always grumbling and complaining. But as long as she fulfilled his needs and performed her duties as a wife he would not throw her out. But it wasn´t fun with her anymore. Come to think of it – it had never been much fun to lie with her. She was a totally frigid creature. No, the fun he needed he got elsewhere. At that thought he looked over at Viktoria, and she looked directly back at him. It was an arrogant look. This not only made him angry, but also sexually aroused.

Meanwhile, Dirtje stood in front of the full milk churns. The cook asked her to quickly bring the churns into the can house, in order to use the quiet day to make some cheese. The small girl struggled to carry them. As she finished she came running, breathless, to the carriage. Harm Reiners was not amused having to wait for her. All three mounted the coach box, and with a crack of the whip the horses started to move. They used the same vehicle as on Viktoria´s trip back from the station a few months ago. Ideal for loading a huge amount of dried peat, but it was more than uncomfortable to sit on. They were thoroughly shaken, rolling over the uneven sandy paths through endless fields and meadows. As Viktoria was sitting in the middle she was thrown from one side to the other and after a few miles every part of her body ached. The farmer took nearly half of the bench so that the ladies had to squeeze together and in the end they held onto one another tightly. Dirtje was obviously enjoying this closeness to Viktoria and smiled at her, she thought what a wonderful day it would be.

The journey through the fields went on and on. The wheat and rye had already been harvested, the stubble-fields shining golden in the sun. Viktoria took a deep breath, taking in the early morning air, full of moisture and the first smell of autumn.

"What is the green stuff in the field over there?" she asked. Reiners looked at her. Then he laughed ironically. "Potatoes, your ladyship! Never seen a potato field before?" Viktoria swallowed, she felt a bit silly. Perhaps she would have recognised the plant at close range, but at this distance? She turned to Dirtje who looked straight ahead and tried to suppress a giggle.

On their journey they passed some lonely farms, saw deep ditches, and crossed canals with Dutch-looking folding bridges. Viktoria took all this in and started to relax. It made such a lovely change to get out and see something different. After a few months her stay at the farm had started to bore her. Perhaps she and Elisabeth should take a day's outing to Norden and have a shopping day. Surely this would please Elisabeth. When Viktoria was still living in Hannover the two had done that, looking in shop windows at the latest fashion in dresses and hats. Afterwards they had relaxed at a coffee house and treated themselves to a piece of gateau with real cream. She would have enjoyed a piece of that right now. But in East Frisia they didn´t seem to go for gateau or even cake. The only thing they ate was a white bread with raisins which they called Krintstuut. This was served with butter like normal bread. And on special occasions the children were given a little spoon of sugar on top. Oh, the memories of Hannover with its elegant way of life made her choke. She pushed them out of her mind.

Next they crossed the little river Abelitz and the village of Marienhafe came into sight with its huge church tower. The settlement was larger than she'd thought as they rumbled through the main street. Viktoria saw the shops and even two department stores. Then they turned right and followed a broad sandy lane downhill. The horses increased their speed but Reiners pulled the reins tighter so the large black Frisians had to slow down. When the carriage passed the last houses the landscape changed. Now there were more bushes and trees. Every so often they passed little cottages and the huts of the poorer farm workers. The further they got, the wilder the area became. The sun was already standing high now and the air shimmering.

After about three miles they arrived at the village of Rechtsupweg. The carriage was passing a pub, a small village school and a shop, they turned left into a small and overgrown lane which seemed to go on forever. Deep ruts made it difficult to pass and the potholes made the carriage creak and swing dangerously. They turned a last time and a ramshackle hut came into view. The windows and door of the mud building were slightly crooked, the roof thatched and light blue smoke came from the chimney.

As soon as the carriage had stopped the door of the hut opened and a mass of children spilled out. Dirtje jumped down from the vehicle and greeted her siblings. Then the kids noticed Viktoria who had also jumped down from the coach box and they stood in awe. Never before had they seen such a beautiful woman. Never such a dress in such blue and then the hat... Viktoria looked at them, dirty, snotty-nosed and dressed in rags, their feet black with dirt. What poverty! But, she had to acknowledge that the children seemed cheerful and happy.

Then Dirtje´s mother joined them, went straight to Harm Reiners, greeting him first, then Viktoria and then her daughter. She took a good look at her.

"You have grown a bit since last year," she commented with tight lips. "But still far too thin." She turned to the farmer. "My girl doesn´t get enough to eat. Or does she have to work so hard that she cannot gain some weight?" She speared him with her eyes. But he laughed and turned away. Always the same accusations, he thought, grinning. "Where is your husband? I want to load quickly. Haven't got time to stand around and tittle-tattle.".

"Hey, just a moment! Before you disappear you have to give me Dirtje´s wages for the last year. And this time all of it! Last year there were three weeks pay missing. Hand it over!" She stood in front of him, her hands on her hips, ready to fight if necessary. Reiners grinned again and pulled a leather purse from this waistcoat pocket and handed it to Eske Bontjes. She greedily grabbed it and counted the coins. All there. Without another word she turned and disappeared into the hut. Reiners remounted, so did Dirtje who called for Viktoria. The vehicle went very slowly now on the way up to the high moor, passing thin birch trees, large areas of heather which were at the end of their bloom and water-filled pot-holes. After a while they reached a plain filled with little towers of brown turf blocks, drying in the wind and sun. They had reached their destination.

Viktoria had never seen such a place. Not far away there was a ten foot high dark brown wall. This was the actual cutting edge. Half way up she saw a wide ledge in the peat where two men were working, cutting rectangular pieces out of the peat. As he saw the carriage arriving, Dirtje's father stopped his work and came to greet them. First of all he embraced his daughter, then shyly greeted the elegant woman standing behind his girl. In the meantime Reiners turned the vehicle so that – after loading- – they would be able to set off more easily with their heavy freight. As Reiners finished he walked to the drying place and checked pieces of turf at random by weighing them in his hands, checking if they were really dry already or perhaps wet. This would be important to the amount they would be able to load. The dryer they were, the more he could transport.

Dirtje looked out for her brother, he was still cutting. She called him. Finally he put his spade into the peat and came towards her with outstretched arms. "My dear little sister! It is so good to see you again. Come here and get a kiss from your favourite brother!" It was a happy re-union. Dirtje turned around to Viktoria. The maid introduced her. "This is Miss Brendel, the cousin of Elisabeth Reiners. She is living with us now, looking after the children on the farm." Viktoria stepped towards Johannes and reached out her hand. "Hello, nice to meet you." He also stretched his hand out but then decided otherwise. "Sorry, I better not give you my hand, it´s very dirty. But I am pleased to meet you too!" Victoria looked into his boyish face. He was sun-tanned, had long blond hair and incredibly green eyes. She had never seen such an eye colour before. He looked at her boldly. And she liked that.

Meanwhile Harm Reiners and father Bontjes had come to a financial arrangement and money had changed hands. Now they could start loading. Dirtje and Viktoria helped too, loading the turf onto wheel-barrows, bringing it to the carriage and handing each piece to Johannes who stacked them tightly onto the loading deck. And whilst everybody worked, Harm Reiners used the time to eat and drink. With a bottle of beer in one hand he watched the women, who – although nearly out of breath by now – were laughing and joking. He snorted disapprovingly.

Then some of the older Bontjes children arrived to help. One boy named Ocko carried a bucket of water for the horses. The loading made good progress and the carriage was nearly half filled as mother Bontjes arrived at the site.

"Eleven o´clock. Time for a cuppa." She walked off briskly and everybody started to follow. She looked back and instructed the children to stay by the horses. Disappointed, they turned back. Only Ocko disap-peared unnoticed into the bushes. He was more than experienced in doing so.

The group took places on a wobbly bench and stools around a small table. Eske Bontjes had put tea cups on the table and poured the tea into them. Viktoria admired the cups. They were made of fine porcelain and painted with a lovely rose design. She hadn´t expected such an elegant tea set in this wilderness. Dirtje's mother seemed to have read Viktoria's mind and grinned. "Well, my dear, even we have some culture here although we are poor. My former employer gave those cups to me for my wedding. It was long ago, but they are still all in one piece. Have to hide them from the little beggars. Otherwise they would be lying in the pit by now." She chuckled and looked at Dirtje. "Now she is old enough she can join us for the posh tea. And she hopefully knows how to behave. Am I right, Harm Reiners? She is a good girl, isn´t she?" Harm Reiners muttered something into his cup. Viktoria saw Dirtje´s face turn to stone and she seemed to shrink.

After the third cup of tea – which was the custom here – they all got up at once and walked back to continue their work. As it got hotter the work seemed harder. But Viktoria felt wonderful, for the first time in ages she felt good all over. In Hannover she had secretly worked in the garden until all her muscles ached. When her father found out he just shook his head, but he never stopped her. As long as she was happy he was happy.

Every time Viktoria came back with her wheelbarrow to the carriage she looked at Johannes and he grinned back. How could she start a conversation with him? "Have you been working on the moor for long?" she dared to ask. He thought for a moment. "Well, here I help now and then, my parents wouldn´t manage without me. But normally I am employed by the company as a driver of the rail carts. I can lay rail-tracks too and service the junctions. That is much easier than the work here, and better paid too."

Eventually the carriage was loaded up high. Suddenly Reiners appeared again out of the nearby bushes and walked around his carriage, inspecting the load. He seemed pleased, Johannes had loaded everything evenly and it was all well-stacked.

Just as the two women fell onto the grass nearby, unpacking their picnic, Harm Reiners gave the order to climb up and leave. "You can eat and drink on the way" he roared. "So, move and get up here. Now!" Dirtje was just about to jump up when Viktoria stopped her. She looked at Reiners. "We just need a brief rest. And when we've had something to drink and a bite to eat we will gladly join you. We should have enough time for that!" Harm Reiners wasn´t used to getting answered back and his puffy face turned crimson. "Damn you! If I say we go then we go. No woman tells me what to do!"

Viktoria stayed calm and continued to eat and drink. But Dirtje had lost her appetite and sat next to Viktoria with her head down. This wasn´t good. This wasn´t good at all! Panic crept up inside her.

After the little break Viktoria packed everything together and stored the basket under the coach bench, next to her bag. The horses had already been made ready to leave with the help of the children. Viktoria took the place in the middle again, Dirtje next to her on the outside. They waved everybody good-bye, the whip gave the start and the heavy vehicle started to move. Both horses snorted at the unexpected weight they had to pull. Slowly they found their rhythm. As they passed the little hut there was nobody to be seen. Dirtje was disappointed, she would have loved to have given a last wave. Who knew when she would see them all again.

They hadn´t gone far when Viktoria suddenly screamed out. Dirtje saw Harm Reiners' hand under Viktoria's skirt between her legs. Viktoria was shocked and tried to move his hand away. But the farmer only laughed at her. "Don´t be such a prude. I think you really like it." Holding the reins with one hand he quickly moved her skirt up further and moved his hand even higher up. Viktoria now tried to fight him off more violently and she yelled at him to stop. But he didn´t. Dirtje had turned to stone. Could she do anything to stop this man? She knew him. He took what he wanted and if one resisted he would hit out without mercy.

"Stop! Stop right now". Viktoria kept on screaming. She tried to get up but at the same time he got up and pulled her from the carriage, then pushed her onto the grass. Viktoria screamed and tried to scramble away but he was stronger. Then he threw himself on top of her and held her down, holding both her hands above her head whilst he tried to pull down her knickers. When he had done so he clumsily unbuttoned his trousers. Viktoria turned her head sideways. She knew what was coming next and closed her eyes. The very same moment she heard a dull noise, felt a sudden jerk in the body on top of her. Harm Reiners made a strange noise. As she dared to open her eyes again she saw blood trickling from his head right onto her face. In panic she screamed again. Reiners gave a rattling sound again and his weight on her felt like a sack of flour holding her to the ground. Only with great difficulty was she eventually able to push him off. A few steps away stood Dirtje, holding a bloody log in her hands. Full of fear she stared at the man on the grass who was writhing in agony. In a second Viktoria stood next to the shocked girl. Dirtje dropped the log and threw herself into Viktoria´s arms. Both were sobbing by now. Neither of them said a word. What could they say? There were no words for all this.

Suddenly Johannes appeared, out of breath. He had heard the screaming and immediately run towards it. He looked at the man on the ground and then at his sister and Viktoria and the blood-stained log on the grass. Dirtje turned and ran into his arms, shaking badly.

"I had to do something! He was hurting her! I had to help her…" and with that she fainted and sank to the ground.

Seeing this, Viktoria´s mind became clear again and she told Johannes what had happened. She didn´t spare on the details. Why should she be embarrassed? She didn´t do anything wrong. Johannes listened and all the while he was looking at Reiners, twisting and groaning on the ground. He had never felt such hate and disgust before.

Viktoria had to think. "What are we going to do with him? He will need a doctor. Perhaps I can clean the wound and put a bandage around his head. And then we have to take him somewhere they can really help him. I have assisted my father long enough to know that he is seriously injured. We have to be quick."

"Eh, and what about Dirtje?" Johannes was speechless. They both turned to the girl who was still lying in the same place. Johannes knelt next to her and lifted her head. Viktoria took a look and calmed him down. "She has only fainted. I'll go and get the little bottle of smelling-salts from my bag, that will bring her back in no time at all." And off she went to the coach box to fetch her emergency bag.

Nobody noticed, just at this moment, that Harm Reiners had scrambled back to his feet and lurched towards Viktoria, who had turned her back on him. But he missed her by a yard and tumbled down against the back leg of one of the horses. The black Frisian kicked out and hit his shoulder which made him fall down onto the ground. In shock both horses neighed and reared, then started to flee, pulling the carriage forward and rolling over the chest of the farmer who gave an eerie shriek. They heard a crack of bones and then it all mingled with the noise of neighing horses, hooves on sandy ground and the creaking coach which disappeared rapidly into the distance.

Johannes had watched everything, he jumped up and ran after the carriage. He had to stop the horses in order to save their lives and the load. Here in the moors this could all end with fatalities. But somebody had apparently been faster. As he came closer he saw that the horses had stopped. Johannes couldn´t believe his eyes. His little brother Ocko sat on the coach-box and grinned at him, the reins tight in his hands.

"I was just on my way to the village when I saw the horses come running so I jumped up and stopped them." He proudly pointed at the hand brake. "You are a real hero. Thank you so much," Johannes panted. Then he went to see to the horses and tried to calm them down. They were still nervous and snorted wildly. He stroked their heads and talked soothingly to them until they calmed down.

What was to be done now? Johannes´s mind ran wild. Reiners was definitely dead. They couldn´t load him onto the carriage – not on top of the peat. They could not arrive back at the farm like that. Or should he send for the police? After all, this was an accident. He paced up and down trying to think .There would be questions, questions which might implicate his sister. No, the best thing was to go back to the scene of the accident and talk to the women. Perhaps Miss Brendel would know what to do. He ordered Ocko to stay with the horses and walked back to the scene of the catastrophe.

Viktoria stood right next to the dead body. She had taken the blue scarf from her hair and had placed it over Reiners' face. That way she wouldn´t have to look at his terrible face. Flies had already gathered on the blood. Then she picked up the blood-stained log and threw it into a watery hole next to the path, so that it was hidden by the long grass on the edge.

"Where is Dirtje?" Johannes looked around but couldn´t see her. "Oh, she has recovered and is now fetching your parents. They will have to bring a blanket so that we can wrap Reiners up and take him home quickly." Viktoria had taken charge.

"But we cannot put him on top of our load, can we?"

He was still uncertain. Dirtje returned with her parents and two of the older boys. They all stood around the dead body and stared. Then his mother unrolled the old brown blanket and placed it over the deceased.

After a short discussion they had found a solution for the transport problem. The two boys were sent to a neighbour nearby who owned a small cart and an old horse. He surely would be willing to take on the job of transporting the body back to the Krummhoern. This way he could earn a little money that day, and any opportunity to do so was welcome. No matter what the load might be.

Chapter 7

The cook had just returned from the chicken coop with a basket full of eggs when she saw the carriage arriving. It was driven by a young man she didn´t know. Next to him sat Miss Brendel and Dirtje. Why was that? What did it mean? Then a second carriage followed. The driver, a scruffy looking old man, got down and gazed around. Then he walked over to Johannes who had jumped down from his carriage. "Okay, here we are. And now?" the old man looked at Johannes. He had to think. What would be best? He called Viktoria and asked her to fetch the lady of the house. She should carefully explain to her what had happened, and that it would be best if the children stayed indoors for the moment. They shouldn't see what the second vehicle contained. Viktoria got down from the coach box and walked slowly to the front door. What would she tell Elisabeth? How should she explain the circumstances? Taking a deep breath she entered the farmhouse.

The cook had come closer in the meantime and looked curiously at the load in the second carriage. Something was lying there, wrapped up in a blanket. Then she saw the boots and she knew what it was. She turned in shock and ran back to the kitchen. Tears ran down her cheeks. In the kitchen she banged the basket with the eggs on the table which made the two maids jump. They looked at her, they had never seen her cry before. "Get me a Schnapps, now!" she sobbed. The girls stood frozen, unable to move. "I need a Schnapps! Get me a large glass. You never believe what I just saw. Out there is the farmer, wrapped up in a blanket. I know it´s him, I'd recognise his boots anywhere. And he is dead!" The girls filled a glass and gave it to the cook. She emptied it in one go, took the bottle and refilled her glass. What a nightmare, she thought and wiped her face with the apron.

Viktoria stood in the hallway and held her cousin tight. She had told her what had happened, an accident, not mentioning what had led up to it. She just couldn´t tell Elisabeth that while she was in a fragile state. Viktoria tried to comfort Elisabeth but to her surprise Elisabeth had pushed her away, run to the door and outside to the yard. As she reached the second carriage with the body she lifted the blanket carefully and looked into her husband's face. Viktoria was glad that she had closed the eyes of the dead man and cleaned the blood from his face before returning here. He looked peaceful, one could think he was just asleep. Looking at him Elisabeth suddenly straightened her shoulders. Why couldn't she cry? In her heart was no pain. No regret. There was no feeling at all.

"Best you bring him indoors right away and put him on the table in the parlour. We have to call for the doctor, he will have to give a death certificate. And we will have to inform the parson." Elisabeth had spoken with a strong voice. Everybody looked at her in surprise. She called for the farmhands who carried the dead body into the house.

Viktoria had gone to her room in the meantime and changed her stained dress. She chose a dark one now of plain cotton, suitable for this occasion. Then she took a black smock. Looking in the mirror she saw her pale face. Her hair was hanging wildly around her head. It had to be fixed too. Whatever had happened, she had to function now. And she had to hide Dirtje when the doctor arrived. It would be best if the girl stayed in her chamber and was not seen by anybody. Perhaps the girl should rest. Viktoria went to the door but turned back and took a black scarf from the dresser to cover the mirror.

An hour later the doctor arrived. He was led into the parlour where Reiners was lying. He examined the body, asked Viktoria to tell him about the exact circumstances of the events that led to the death and muttered something now and then. Again and again he looked at the wound on the head. Victoria stuck to her version of the story. Reiners had suddenly stumbled at the carriage and fallen against the horses, they had kicked out at him and started to flee and somehow the farmer had slipped under the wheels of the carriage. The wheels had crushed his chest.

The doctor looked briefly over the edge of his reading glasses at Viktoria. She felt most uncomfortable at this. But then he signed the death certificate and handed it to Elisabeth who silently stood by the door. "Please accept my sincere condolences. It must be hard for you and the family. Would you like me to give you something to calm your nerves?" Elisabeth shook her head. He took his bag and left without saying good-bye. The women looked at each other. Had he believed them? Or had he become suspicious? Would he inform the police?

Elisabeth regained control of herself and gave orders. The dead body had to be washed, then she would dress him in his best Sunday suit ready for the funeral. Viktoria would have to assist her. And she would have to talk with the cook about the wake. She didn't know how many neighbours and family would take part. And what should be offered to eat and drink on an occasion like that? She had no idea herself. Oh, and she had to inform Harm Reiners' brother who lived in the Groningerland in the Netherlands. "When is the parson coming? Oh my God. I have forgotten the funeral director!" Elisabeth ran briskly into the kitchen and Viktoria couldn't believe that this was her cousin – the feeble woman had come alive again. The cook was also surprised to see Elisabeth like that. The farmer's wife seemed – for the first time since she had arrived at the farm years ago – to have taken the reins into her hands and behave as was expected of her.

The same evening the traditional wake was held. Some of the neighbours came. Most of them were polder farmers like Reiners with their wives. The men had gathered around the open coffin in the parlour, drinking beer and schnapps and later on in the evening their laughter could be heard as they told stories about the deceased. This was a local tradition. Part of remembrance and even gratitude. Whilst the men were having a good time the women sat with sour faces in the kitchen having tea and biscuits. Every so often they looked at Elisabeth in pity which made her very uncomfortable. She poured tea as often as she could to have some purpose here. When would this wretched evening come to an end? Elisabeth had never met these women before and decided that she didn't like them with their false pity for her bereavement. Viktoria, sitting next to her, must have read her thoughts and stroked her arm gently, which made Elisabeth burst into tears and leave the room. All eyes followed her.

On the day of the funeral it was pouring with rain. The church service had been planned for the early afternoon and long before it began the church filled to the last seat. Harm Reiners was a well-liked man in this area and a longstanding member of the church elders. Even though he hardly ever attended the services. But nobody wanted to miss a funeral like this. It was the duty of any Christian person to give him a good send-off. To show respect for the widow and the poor children who sat in the first pew. Right behind them were all the maids and farm helpers, together with the cook, who was sobbing loudly.

At the end of the funeral everybody was invited to tea and cake at the local public house. Then the family returned home. Most farmers stayed on and ordered beer and schnapps. Discussions about the deceased began and got heated until some men started to fight and fists flew. The landlord watched calmly and smiled. There was nothing like a good fight after a funeral. This cleared the air. He got back behind the bar and pulled the next pint.

Chapter 8

Three days after the funeral a coach was made ready for Elisabeth and Viktoria to see the solicitor in Emden. Hearing about the death of Harm Reiners he had come to the funeral and afterwards had arranged the appointment for them. All presumptive heirs were invited. This announcement puzzled Viktoria. Who, apart from Elisabeth and her children were heirs to the farm? So she insisted to come along and make sure that things were properly conducted.

The two women arrived in town a little late. The coach driver dropped them outside an impressive Renaissance building right next to the Delft, a former little harbour basin in the centre of town. The solicitor's office was on the first floor with a beautiful view onto the water.

In the reception office a young clerk was waiting for them. He didn´t look pleased.

"How dare you be late for an appointment like this? The advocate is waiting and not amused." He stalked over to a huge wooden door and knocked. As he opened the door he took one step back and waved with an exaggerated gesture for the women to enter. Viktoria looked at him. Such arrogance at such a young age? Silly man, she thought.

The advocate sat behind an enormous wooden desk, he lifted his head and frowned. Somebody was already sitting before him. Both women were surprised. As the man turned Elisabeth gave a little cry. It was the brother of Harm Reiners. She had only met him once at her wedding as he lived in the Groninger-land in West Frisia, and although she had invited him and his wife to the funeral he hadn´t appeared. But perhaps the message hadn´t reached him in time.

They greeted each other and sat down. The young clerk was instructed to bring an additional chair for Viktoria. Then the advocate spoke. First of all he gave his condolences to everybody and pulled a sealed letter out of his desk drawer and put it onto the table in front of him. His eyes moved around looking at each of them intensely.

"We have gathered here today to read out the Last Will and Testament of Harm Reiners. It was his wish and it is my duty to act on his behalf. He was a long-standing client of mine. He gave this to me six months ago." He took the letter, broke the wax seal and un-folded the paper. Then he read:

"I , Harm Menno Reiners, born on the 3rd of February 1863 in Upleward, Krummhoern, now living at the Rein-ers Farm, Greetsiel, married, declare, in full possession of my mind, the following in case of my death:

My entire farm belongings, including the house and stables, barns as well as all fields and meadows and all livestock I leave to my brother, Jan Reiners, presently resident of Groningerland, to hold in trust for my son who will inherit all on his twenty-fifth birthday. I wish for Jan Reiners and his Dutch wife Hendrike to have custody of my son and to reside at the farm. I further instruct that all members of staff are to be kept on, on the same conditions as at the time of my death. To my wife, Elisabeth Sophia, nee Brendel, as well as my two daughters Uda and Feemke , I leave a one-off payment of two hundred marks each from my cash deposit. They must leave the farm within one month and must forfeit the right to return thereafter.

One last sentence to my wife: You were not a good wife for me nor a good mother for my only son and heir. I wish you and the girls all the best for your future, perhaps a life in a big town. You never belonged in the countryside. Now you will have to work for your living. Signed and certified...etc. etc."

The Advocate pushed the letter across the table. Immediately Jan Reiners grabbed it and read it again. "Now that´s a surprise!" He turned to Elisabeth and grinned "Oh, I don´t believe it. Just what I needed right now! My old girl at home will go crazy when she hears this. She always wanted a farm for herself with servants she could order around. Oh, today is my lucky day!" He jumped up and down with excitement.

Elisabeth had turned white. This could not be true! Viktoria looked at the advocate. "But, this cannot be right? To take everything from a wife and the girls, and to take her son from her and to send them off with a laughable amount. We'll fight this Will. I know some very good solicitors in Hannover. This is not the last of it. This is ridiculous."

Suddenly Elisabeth jumped up. "Viktoria, let's go! Leave this cretin with the farm and the vindictive little child. My son is already as evil as his dad was. He is mean and false. No, I lost him a long time ago. Although I tried again and again, but Harm's influence was stronger. Let him stay at the farm. My girls and I are free now. So are you. We can live anywhere we want. Come on, let's go." She pulled Viktoria by the sleeve, out of the office and past the clerk, outside, onto the street.

"Oh, Elisabeth? What have you done just now?" Viktoria started crying. Elisabeth answered calmly: "What I should have done years ago – leave and live a free life. You know, it wasn´t really a life with that man."

The whole morning there was a high tension at the farm. Most of all the cook had speculated what might happen to the farm now that the farmer was dead. They didn´t know what could have been stated in the last Will, surely there would be major changes now the farmer was gone. But what changes? Would the farmer's wife be in charge from now on? The thought horrified her. She's no good for anything. One could only hope that she – when the year of mourning was over- would marry again quickly. It needed a man to run the farm. If by that time there was anything left of it. Elisabeth Reiners didn´t have a clue about farming and even less about book-keeping The cook went back into the kitchen and got the bottle out. Only a little one, she told herself, to calm her nerves. Soon she was joined by the farmhands. The maids were ordered out of the room and told to carry on with their work.

When they finally heard a coach pulling up they all ran outside. Full of anticipation they stood there in line and waited. First the children and Dirtje were sent indoors. Whatever was said now wasn´t meant for children's ears.

Elisabeth and Viktoria stepped down from the coach. The coach driver joined the others. Elisabeth looked around. Everybody was here – except Dirtje. Just as well. Good. Well, she had to do it now. Tell everybody. As soon as it was out it would be reality. Then she started to tell the tale.

Later that evening Dirtje and the girls were informed. That night nobody slept well. What would the future bring?

Chapter 9

After the shock of the previous events Viktoria and Elisabeth were thinking about the possibilities of the future they now faced. Viktoria thought of a return to Hannover. She loved that town with its theatres and cafes. But was it such a good idea? There were also the painful memories.

Elisabeth suggested they go back to her home town Oldenburg. But she no longer knew many people there. Her parents were dead and most of her girlfriends had married and moved away as she had done. A few remaining contacts had ceased with her move to the Krummhoern. "When I come to think about it, we could go anywhere. Even to America or Canada. Now, that would be a real new start." Only a few weeks ago she had read an article in the local newspaper which told the story of some East Frisians who had emigrated to America. It hadn´t been just one family but half the village had gone. They travelled to Hamburg and from there boarded a ship to New York. But they already had family members over there. In their case relatives in Iowa who had vouched for them. This had made it much easier to be allowed into the country. Viktoria had to admit that she'd started to like the idea. She turned to her cousin. "But there is one problem. They speak English over there. Do you speak any English?" Elisabeth shook her head. "But a little bit of French which I learned at school. My mum thought it more appropriate. She explained that even in Russia all people of some standing would speak French. I had no choice. But surely, I could learn English when I am over there."

Viktoria raised her eyebrows. "Of course, you could. But it would be much better if all of us spoke some English already before entering the country. Just think about the immigration officials we might have to argue with." This seemed a good enough reason for Elisabeth. "Okay, then let´s start the lessons right away."

Dirtje passed the table in the parlour where Viktoria, Elisabeth and the girls were sitting. What were they doing there? They were speaking funny words she'd never heard before. So she asked about it. When she heard that they were learning a new language because the family were going to live in America she started to cry. "But you cannot leave me here! I can't stay here on the farm without you! Please take me with you. I will do anything, I could wash your clothes, do the cleaning and cooking – but do not leave me here."

Elisabeth and Viktoria exchanged a look. Dirtje was right. It could be dangerous for her to stay at the farm. Not to mention that she might one day tell somebody, even by mistake, what really happened on the moors. She would end up in prison. They had to take her, there was no doubt.

Viktoria considered. "If we use some of the money from the sale of the house in Hannover to make a start over there it should be enough for Dirtje too. What do you think, Elisabeth? Is she going to join us?" Elisabeth had tears in her eyes and looked at the distraught girl. "Of course you can come with us. Now then, you'd better sit down and join the lessons." Dirtje ran into

Elisabeth´s arms, then into Viktoria´s. Now she only had to get the permission of her parents. So they decided to visit them the coming Sunday. They promised they would take the girls and have a picnic to make it seem like a treat. After all, going past the place of the terrible event would not be easy.

Everything went well. They reached the little hut and Uda and Feemke stared in total disbelief that humans could live like that. But then they met the children and soon went off to have some adventures. In the meantime Dirtje's parents sat outside discussing the plans for America with their visitors. Her parents were understandably reluctant but wished her well. Just then Johannes arrived back from the moor and was surprised to see his sister there in the company of Elisabeth and Viktoria. Now he knew where the prettily dressed girls he had seen with his siblings had come from. When he heard about the plans he gulped. Of all his siblings Dirtje was closest to his heart. But such was life. Some day they all went to live their own lives. And if they were clever it would be far away from the poverty and hard toil he had to contend with. "When will you be leaving?" he asked carefully.

It was Viktoria who answered. "Early next month. When we find a ship. I have already done some research, we could go from Bremerhaven or from Hamburg. There are different destinations but most emigrants want to go to New York. From there we could travel on, perhaps to Iowa where there are already many communities with people from East Frisia. We wouldn´t be so alone there and perhaps it will help us to make a good start."

Father Bontjes wanted more information. " Where is this land Iowa?" Viktoria had studied the map of America. "Very far to the west of the continent. It seems as flat as East Frisia and has fertile land good for farming."

At this Elisabeth looked up in horror. This information was not to her liking. She would rather stay in New York and enjoy a more cultured life. But she said nothing for now.

Father Bontjes scratched his bald head. "In the middle of nowhere then? It'll mean that you will probably marry farmers and toil like now? What´s the point of that, eh? But it´s your choice. I definitely couldn´t live there, I would miss the sea and the fresh salty air. No, not for me I´d say." He snorted in disapproval. Women! He just hoped that they would look after this daughter.

One week later Elisabeth and Viktoria went back to Emden. They first went to the bank where they had made an appointment regarding the transferral of money to America. They didn´t want to have to carry large sums of cash with them on the journey in case they got robbed. But the manager ensured them there would not be any problems. They just had to send a telegram to him. Then they drew out an amount of cash for the first few weeks over there. With that they would pay for the passage and for food on board ship.

Afterwards, they had to see the advocate one last time to sign some final papers. It took him by complete surprise when he found out that the women would soon be leaving the country to go to America. What a courageous decision, he congratulated them.

" Where are you taking a ship from? Perhaps you don´t know but there are ships from Emden to America." Elisabeth and Viktoria hadn´t known this. "No, we didn´t know. That would be perfect." The advocate smiled.

"By coincidence just this morning I talked to the captain of a ship here in the harbour. It is the steam ship "Concordia". He crosses the ocean on a regular route up to North America with his freighter. And as far as I know he takes passengers as well. They are loading right now and intend to set off the day after tomorrow. You´ll find the ship on the commercial dock. If I were you I would drive there right away and ask if you can have a passage. Or is that too soon?" Both women looked at each other in total surprise. Elisabeth spoke first. "Well, to be honest, that is very sudden. But perhaps destiny. We will drive there right away and inquire. The coach is waiting just outside."

The advocate stretched out his hands to them. "Well then, all the best for you all. I wish you luck for a new start. Life is full of opportunities when you are open to them. Look after yourselves and let me know how you are getting on over there."

Advocate Meyerdirks watched the women get into the coach and drive off in the direction of the harbour. He smiled. This time would be really profitable for the captain Redenius. He had sent him enough passengers. And his cut would be – as ever- rewarding for him.

As the two women stepped onto the street they looked at each other. They should take this chance. They asked the coachman to do a detour to the harbour before returning home. Soon they found the right ship which was larger than anticipated. Next to it stood a man in uniform. He watched the loading of some goods. As he heard the coach approaching he turned in surprise. Two women got out and walked towards him.

"Are you the captain of this ship?" Elisabeth looked him right in the eye. "Who wants to know?" Came the answer. "The Advocate Meyerdirks sent us. We are looking for a passage to America. Which harbours are you visiting?" He smiled and made a bow. "Captain Redenius, please to meet you. Well, normally we take the straight route to Boston and New York. But this time we have to unload some freight at Halifax in Canada first. How many places do you need?"

"Well, we are two adults, one teenager and two children aged eight and ten. How much does it cost?" He calculated in his head. "One hundred and sixty marks per person. This is for a decent cabin and the food for twelve days. The price is the same for every passenger, they all sleep and eat. No bargaining about this." That was a shock. It was expensive, much more than they would have had to pay from Hamburg or Bremerhaven. But, so they reckoned, it had the advantage that they could go from Emden and didn´t have to travel far to reach a ship. It was well-known that because of the high number of emigrants some long waiting times occurred which also cost money. A long discussion began. But finally they agreed to the terms. The captain seemed pleased.

"The ship leaves the day after tomorrow at eight in the morning. Be there on time. Per family you can take one sea-chest and each person may carry two pieces of luggage, it doesn't matter if they are cases or bags. They are kept in the cabin, the trunk goes into the freight area. All luggage must have a tag with name and address of where you have come from and where you are going to. This is for the customs on the other side. And I advise on warm clothes for the journey, good boots and woolly caps or scarves. It is the beginning of September and over there it can get very cold. Oh yes, and definitely no hats for the ladies. They will be in the ocean in no time at all. That's it for now. You pay after you have boarded the ship and before we set off. And now you will have to excuse me, I have work to do. See you the day after tomorrow." He turned and went back to surveying the loading of freight.

Viktoria saw him walk away. "Oh, Elisabeth, what have we just done? " Elisabeth took her into her arms. "We are going to America. To a new life." Then they both jumped up and down squealing with excitement.

The captain looked back at the silly women. Yes, now they were laughing, but soon they would be sea sick. He grinned.

The coachman had witnessed everything and raised his eyebrows. All this didn't feel right somehow. He didn't like the look of this captain. No, not at all.

When they returned to the farm a big surprise was waiting for them. Next to the front door stood two carriages, highly stacked with furniture, baskets and bundles. Jan Reiners had arrived with his wife Hendrike. Everybody was busy unloading. Hendrike, a sturdy female of about forty, supervised the farmhands and maids who busily ran to and fro with boxes and pieces of furniture. Even Elisabeth´s daughters were carrying heavy baskets into the house. The little boy Enno stood dangerously near to the horses and threw pebbles at them. The Groningers didn´t take any notice of him. Elisabeth rushed to the child and pulled him away. That could have ended badly. She hoped the couple would take better care of him in the future.

Jan and Hendrike said a brief hello. Hendrike gave them an accusing look. "About time! Where were you? There is chaos here with all those useless people around and you ladies drive around the country amusing yourselves. Get your backsides moving and help with this now!"

This attitude made all of them speechless. No, not us! They marched past Hendrike into the house. Time to go. The sooner they packed the sooner they could leave. Including Dirtje. Shortly after lunch they were ready, said a last good-bye to the staff, then to the new tenants and to little Enno. He didn´t understand what was going on and stood next to Hendrike who held his hand. Elisabeth bent down to kiss him. "Mummy will go now, be a good boy and always listen to auntie Hendrike. She will look after you from now on. I will never forget you and as soon as I can I will write. Don´t forget me, please." She choked on the words. Enno just looked blankly at her.

Now the open carriage was packed and they climbed in. Elisabeth took a last look at the farm as they departed. For more than ten years this had been her home. So many memories but not many good ones. As they left the forecourt they started to look ahead in the direction of Emden and to a new future.

"Where are we going to go? The ship leaves in two days. Do we have to sleep in the harbour, perhaps outside?" Dirtje was worried. But Elisabeth reassured her. "No my dear, we are going to stay at the Central Hotel in Emden until the ship departs. I know the owner, I am sure he will find some room for us. And if not, there will be other hotels."

They had just left the long drive from the farm to the main road when a little carriage with two men appeared in the distance. Somebody was waving like mad. As they came closer Dirtje started to scream. It was the neighbour from her village and next to him her brother Johannes. They asked the coachman to stop and wait. What did they want? A few minutes later they met. Johannes jumped down and ran to Dirtje. "Oh, I am so happy I got here in time. I am so lucky. He embraced his sister. "I couldn't sleep last night and had a good think. I decided that I will come with you. You will surely need a man at your side to defend you?" He looked at Elisabeth's puzzled face. "Oh, my dear boy. I am afraid that will not be possible. We have already booked the tickets and they are not cheap. You don't have any money, do you?" Johannes grinned at her."- Quite right. But perhaps I can work for my passage on this ship? Let me at least try. And I promise I will not be a burden to you. I want to work. And perhaps you´ll need somebody to protect you over there. Thugs can be everywhere. And apart from all that I promised my dear parents that I would look after my favourite little sister."

This was an unexpected situation, but after a short discussion they nodded their heads. Johannes and Dirtje screamed with joy. Johannes went back to the other coach driver, thanking him again and fetching his linen bag. Then he joined the others. Now it was getting to be a tight squeeze inside the coach. The horses lifted their heads and off they went in the direction of Emden.

Chapter 10

Johannes had slept in a proper bed for the first time in his life. The hotel had offered him and Dirtje a servant's room each. Pure luxury for both of them.

Soon after a big breakfast Johannes ran to the docks. He found the Concordia easily and also the captain who was standing on the dock supervising the loading process again. When he heard the young man's request he wasn´t interested at first, but then he suddenly remembered something the cook had told him earlier and called him back. Apparently there was a problem. The kitchen helper had been taken ill and could not join them on this trip. The cook could not do all the work on his own. Some other help had to be organised at very short notice. So Johannes came at the right moment and after some discussion they agreed on the terms: free passage to America, a bunk in the crew cabin as well as free food. Work started at 6 am and ended after supper at night. His duties would include helping the cook with the preparation of the food, the serving of the meals, and washing all dishes and pots. After all this the kitchen and dining area had to be cleaned. They would have to cook for ten crew and for fourteen passengers on this journey. Johannes felt dizzy. But he nodded at each of the terms. They agreed with a handshake. The captain told him to come on board the very same evening at supper time and report to the Smutje. Looking at Johannes´s puzzled face he had to grin. Smutje, he explained, is what the cook is called on a ship. Ah well, here we had yet another land lubber.

The Smutje was critical of this deal and told the captain. "I hope he doesn't get sea sick as often as the last slob." They both followed Johannes with their eyes as he ran back down the docks towards town again. "At least he can run and I hope it will stay like that. Couldn´t use a lazy fat gannet like the last one again." With that he went back to his work.

They had stayed two nights at the Central Hotel and enjoyed the modest elegance and luxury of the best hotel in town. Now the great day of departure had finally arrived. Johannes had already left the previous evening. Everybody was glad that he could join them, especially his sister. With relief she had started to talk about the journey and got more and more excited about her trip. After all, it was her very first long journey. Just as well, she thought, that Elisabeth and Viktoria had more experience in travelling. They had been on a ship before on their journey to the isle of Norderney in the year 1905. But that trip had only been short. Now they would cross an ocean and stay on board for at least twelve days.

The group arrived on the dock more than an hour early and were not the first passengers waiting. There were little family groups standing tightly together and eyeing each other. Next to them was their luggage. Most of them had only a few small bundles with them. One of the ship's mates came and tried to shift Elisabeth's heavy trunk but to no avail. So he ordered a second man to help him.

Then the passengers were allowed to go on board. Captain Redenius sat in his office and asked one group after another for the fare. He also asked for their documents in order to write the shipping lists. This he would do later on.

Viktoria had already calculated and gave him the exact money. Redenius counted it and looked up at her. "That is not enough. You didn't include the harbour charges and the money for the health check in America." His look became demanding.

"You didn't mention this before. Sorry, how much is it in addition then?"

Redenius looked down at his paperwork. "Per head, twelve marks. Altogether seventy-two." He grinned. Viktoria recalculated. They were only five people, so she told the captain. He replied looking angry now. " Seventy-two my lady. Or will you not pay for the young man to enter America? Fine by me, if he works well he can stay permanently on board. He seems a good worker."

Viktoria gasped. She had forgotten Johannes! "Oh, I do apologise. Of course I will pay the charges for him. But I just have to go outside because my cousin has got the purse. I'll be back in a minute." She turned and left the office. Full of anger she went back to Elisabeth who waited outside. This would be the most costly voyage ever, she grunted. But Elisabeth calmed her down and pulled out the purse from her corset.

Soon afterwards everything had been paid for and the passengers were taken to their cabins on the lower deck. The sailor opened the first the door for the women, then he showed the men where to sleep which was a long way down the narrow hallway at the other end. When they entered they only saw darkness. As their eyes adjusted they looked in surprise at four sets of bunk beds. And three beds had been taken already. They recognised the women from the dock. They also seemed to be in shock looking at the new arrivals.

"Yes, this is how we looked as we were dumped here .We had expected a cabin to ourselves too." It was the woman from the bed next to the door.

"At this price we would have expected something else, too." Came a voice from a dark corner of the room.

Elisabeth and Viktoria looked at each other. No, this was not acceptable. But the girls had already run into the room and taken up two upper bunks on one side. As they all looked closer they saw that the bunks had been made of rough wood but the bedding seemed clean.

"I just hope the mattress is not too hard and filled with itchy straw." Elisabeth inspected the grey looking sack. It would have to do. But it certainly didn´t seem to be of high comfort.

That moment a strong shudder and roar went though the ship's hull. Then the floor started swaying and the women screamed and tried to hold onto anything they could find. The engines now ran at a regular rhythm, from outside they could hear commands to haul in the anchors. The iron colossus started to move.

The woman next to the door jumped up. "The ship is moving! Let's go on deck and take a last look at Emden and East Frisia. I don´t want to miss that down here."

She ran along and knocked on the men's cabin door but nobody answered. "Hey Jan, come out of there. Let's go on deck. We are moving already!" Nothing. So she stormed upstairs.

The others followed her. On deck stood three men and a young boy who looked out at the harbour. They could see many types of ship, wooden fishing vessels, canal barges and many freighters. The smaller ones were probably coastal ones, the larger would have come across the sea. Where did they originate from and where would they be heading to? The girls had great fun reading the names. They passed the Santa Maria from Lisboa, the Clermont from Harwich, the Lisa from Cuxhaven, the Zeehond from Amsterdam and the Madelaine from Brest. This was so exciting! Before the ship could leave the inner harbour they had to pass the Nessmerlander Lock, having done so they entered the estuary of the river Ems which led them out onto the North Sea. After a while the island of Borkum came into sight to starboard.

The passengers stood there, still enjoying the view and the fresh breeze. Slowly the ship started to sway slightly even though the surface of the sea seemed calm. Soon some of the ladies felt nauseous and returned to their cabin with the excuse to get settled and unpack. But on the lower deck they felt even worse and had to lie down – just in case.

Elisabeth and Viktoria had decided to go and see the captain once more and complain about the cabin situation. They asked one of the sailors to show them the way. He led them onto the bridge. They waited by the side door until Redenius arrived.

"Well ladies, what can I do for you this time?" Viktoria gave him a pinched look. "We are not happy with our cabin. As a matter of fact we didn't expect to share a room with so many people. This is not what we have arranged and paid for. We demand a proper cabin for the five of us. Including a wash basin."

Now Redenius´s face turned red. He gave her a nasty look.

"There is no other cabin, I am afraid. If you don't like it you can hop off right now. Perhaps my lady should have booked a first class cabin on one of the Ballin ships in Hamburg. Here we have only one class for all." And with that he turned around and went back to take over the steering. His audacity made Viktoria speechless. But it was too late. Somehow they had to put up with the situation. After all, it was only for twelve days.

As the journey progressed, Elisabeth's face turned paler. "Will you excuse me, please? I think I might have to go and lie down for a while. See you later." And with that she disappeared. Viktoria still felt fine, so did the girls. They walked around, exploring, taking everything in. It was a sunny day with calm waters. Perfect for a trip into the future. Viktoria thought that she should write all this down, perhaps keep a diary. So many new experiences should be recorded.

Long after midday the passengers heard a bell. It was Johannes, running over the deck and shouting that lunch was being served. "One o'clock! Lunch be-ing served in the mess room! All passengers are requested to go there now. Lunch! Lunch!" As he passed Viktoria and the girls he winked at them. "We're serving fish soup and pudding afterwards. And I helped to make it all." Proudly he continued his tour on deck, ringing his bell loudly. Then he moved to the other side of the deck where the men were standing.

The dining area was a well-lit room on the upper deck with four portholes on one side through which they could look out onto the water. It contained four long tables. Along the sides were long benches and at the head of the fixed tables stood wooden chairs with arm rests. All looked comfortable and clean. The passengers admired the shiny wooden table tops which were framed with a slightly higher edge and rounded brass corners. They had never seen such a table before and wondered why they were made like that. Only Hajo Lammers, from Timmel, a boat builder by profession, knew. In admiration he stroked the edges. This was fine craftsmanship.

It took a while until all passengers had taken their places. Even the women from the lower deck had arrived. Then Johannes started to serve. He ran to the serving hatch, took two plates at the time and brought them over to the tables. As they started eating the cook looked out. Everybody seemed to be tucking in. The fish stew was tasty and hot and everybody had a slice of brown bread to go with it.

Only one woman pulled a face at her plate. She hated fish and pushed the plate over to her husband who smiled at her. When the dessert came he gave his portion to her in return. Semolina pudding with red currant juice had never been to his liking. Afterwards tea was being served. The East Frisians scowled when they looked into their mugs — pale water. A decent cup of tea looked different. And there was no cream or sugar in sight. Never mind, they thought to themselves, perhaps they had better get used to it, the sooner the better.

Chapter 11

After lunch the little groups began to introduce themselves to each other. Gerti Janssen made a start. She introduced her husband Jan and her daughter Emmi. Her husband was not very talkative, but Gerti was.

"Well, we heard about the possibility to take a ship from Emden directly to Canada. Our destination is Halifax. My husband worked at the ship yard here in Emden for many years but he lost his job six months ago. As a result we lost our home and moved in with my parents. But that didn´t work out. My father and Jan didn´t get on at all. Just as well that our daughter Emmi had just finished school. When some people told us about New Brunswick we decided that it might be the place for a new life. They are looking for ship builders over there. And now we are here. We heard about the Concordia only last week and are so pleased that we got three passages on this ship." She looked at her husband who nodded.

"Nearly our story." Hinnerk Frerichs looked solemnly onto the table top before him. "I am a fisherman by profession. I worked on my brother's fishing vessel in Greetsiel. But it wasn´t easy to work with him. He gave me hell every single day, he always thought he knew everything better. He nearly ruined the family business, all because he was a heavy drinker."

Gerti Janssen glanced sideways at her husband. He stared into the distance. Yes, the wretched alcohol destroyed so many families. If he hadn´t been drinking so much at work he would still be at the ship yard. He had received enough warnings from the management before they sacked him.

Sina Frerichs stroked her husband's arm. "Hinnerk, it's over now. We are going to America. Your uncle in Iowa has promised that you will find work on one of the farms and that we will get our own house there. He even vouched for us so that we can enter the country without any problems." She gave him an encouraging look. But Hinnerk was not convinced. "Why don't you understand? I don't want to go and live in Iowa. I had a look on the map and it's in the bloody middle of nowhere. Right in the middle of a huge country. And very far from any water. I don't want to end up as a land lubber, I am a sailor." He banged his fist down on the table top."When will you understand this, wife?"

Sina smiled quietly. "Oh, Hinnerk, we don't have to go there. Perhaps we will find something else on our way. Perhaps a nice place by the ocean. To me it doesn't matter at all as long as the two of us are to-gether." Sina took her husband's hand and squeezed it lovingly.

Everybody looked at each other again. At the corner table sat Hajo Lammers with his wife Thalea and son Freerk. Hajo's fingers ran over the raised edge of the table before him. He briefly introduced his family. "I am Hajo Lammers, boat builder from Timmel. My parents have a yard there building wooden sailing ships of all sizes. But as we all know the time for sailing ships is nearly over now that nearly every ship is built from iron and fitted with steam engines, like this one we are sitting on right now. Time is money. Never mind the tradition. I have two more brothers who work at the family yard too. My older brother and I didn't get on either. Last winter we had one of many arguments about the future of the trade when he suddenly attacked me. I nearly lost an eye in the fight. Now my sight is poor. "He pointed at the round glasses on the top of his nose. "So, Thalea and I decided to leave and seek a new adventure in America and hopefully a better future for our son." He turned to look at the ten year old sitting next to him. The boy glowed with excitement.

Now it was Elisabeth's turn. "My name is Elisabeth Reiners, last address Krummhoern, but I come from Oldenburg. I am a widow, my husband died not long ago in an accident. We had a large farm which his brother has now inherited. There was no longer room for me and my daughters Uda and Feemke. This is my cousin Viktoria from Hannover who has joined me. Next to her is Dirtje, a...friend of our family. And the young man who just served lunch to us is her brother Johannes. None of us really knows where this journey will take us but we intend to stay together. I am sure there is a better life ahead."

Everybody nodded at that. This was the high hope of all.

In the late afternoon they passed the Dutch islands on the port side. Now the ship started swaying . As it entered the English Channel the waves became higher and the sea rough. The women went back to the cabin to lie down. When it was time for supper only Elisabeth and Viktoria appeared and a few of the men. They were hungry. The fresh air at sea made them hungry. But after a few bites Elisabeth got up, looking pale again. She swiftly went back below deck.

In the evening they passed the English coast. But the distant lights were only seen by a few. Sea sickness took hold of them, even the men were affected. Only Johannes enjoyed the constant rolling of the ship as he ran across the floor of the mess and the kitchen. He felt on top form. The cook looked at him in admiration.

Many days passed. Everybody knew the routine, the meal times, the daily walks on deck, they stood in small groups and talked about their dreams and worries. The children ran around the ship until the captain had enough of it and ordered the parents to keep them under control, otherwise he would throw them all off at the next harbour.

One day Johannes asked one of the sailors when they would arrive at the next port. The sailor smiled and whispered. "Tomorrow night we will anchor briefly just outside Cork and take a little freight on board in the dark. No time for the pub. And listen to my advice. Don't dare to show your face then, otherwise you will be in trouble with the captain. After that we will cross the Atlantic."

The Irish Sea was even rougher than the Channel. Then the freighter got into calmer waters and soon after the engines stopped. The slight movement lulled everybody to sleep. Therefore nobody noticed the boats which came from the nearby coast of Cork and now sailed towards the ship. A number of long wooden cases were hauled on board. They seemed to be heavy. Then two men scrambled their way up the side of the hull on a rope ladder. The captain took them below deck. Meanwhile the wooden cases were brought down into the food store where they were piled up in the far corner. The cook watched with eagle eyes. As the last box was stacked he placed boxes of vegetables and sacks of potatoes on top. With a bit of luck the customs at the next harbours wouldn´t look closely at the pantry. He took a last look. It was perfect. He only hoped that the new kitchen help wouldn´t be too curious.

As soon as the boats were empty they disappeared back into the dark, the ship's engines started up again and the freighter started to move. From now it would take another nine to twelve days, depending on how rough the sea was. Back in his cabin the captain studied the route once more. Everything was going according to plan. He got his pipe out. This would be his last trip on this or any other ship to North America. After this he would have made enough money to retire. Retire in style. He would buy himself a little cottage somewhere along the coast in Germany, perhaps even a captain's house on the river Elbe in Hamburg. He should have enough for that. This had always been his secret dream.

The next morning everybody wondered about the two men who were sitting in the far corner drinking tea. They spoke quietly to each other. Viktoria tried to listen, it was English but with a strange accent she couldn´t quite understand. Or was it a different language altogether? Where did they suddenly come from? She hadn't seen them before. Were they part of the crew? No, they looked more like passengers. Did they have an extra cabin? This was all very strange.

Later, on deck, she stood next to Johannes and asked him about the two men. He didn´t know where they had come from either. It was a mystery to him as well. Perhaps it had something to do with the wooden boxes in the food store? When he'd asked the cook about them he'd been very angry and told Johannes to mind his own business, otherwise he would regret it. This was warning enough for him. Something strange was going on here. And now these two new passengers had appeared. Something was wrong here. But, he told himself, soon they would be in America and it would be better not to know more. Johannes took a deep breath. He advised Viktoria in a whispered voice not to investigate further.

The passengers had just started eating their soup when the ship suddenly lurched to one side. A high wave had hit them sideways. All the freshly filled plates slid across the table, only held by the raised edges. But the hot contents poured over the edge and spilt onto the clothes of the passengers. The women jumped up screaming loudly, the hot liquid had scalded their skin. The children also cried. Only the men were not affected because of the thick, woolly layers of clothes they were wearing. Johannes rushed over, trying to help wipe the soup from the women's dresses. But they pushed him away indignantly refusing his attempts to assist them. They ran downstairs into the cabin to get their dresses off and look at the burnt skin. Viktoria helped them undress and searched in her emergency bag for an ointment. She had made it herself. It could help with the burns but not against the pain. So the women started to cry and moan. That night not many of them found their sleep.

In the following days it had become very quiet in the mess. Hardly anybody attended at meal times. The sea had become so rough that even the men had started to pray secretly. They didn´t want to die at sea. They didn´t want to die at all. The freighter was thrown around like a nut shell, hour after hour. They all hoped it would be over soon. The sea sickness took a further toll. The two cabins were stinking of vomit, and the buckets which they used to relieve themselves in, kept falling over, spilling the contents on the floor. Through the movement of the ship the liquids ran everywhere. Viktoria, being the fittest of them all, tried her best to clean the place several times a day and Johannes helped her. He took care of the men's cabin. When would it get better? Most of the women and children were so weak that they stayed in bed and soiled their beds. Viktoria started to get really worried about the situation. If they were not careful they would all become seriously ill. And this could mean no entry to America, which would be disastrous. She remembered her father telling her he'd been on a ship in the tropics where many people had died of Cholera. She had to do more than cleaning and washing sheets. Cold, soapy water wasn´t going to be enough. She looked at her red and cracked hands. Tears were in her eyes.

Later she went on deck to look for the drying sheets and covers when the captain suddenly appeared next to her. "Considering you are such a fine lady you are doing surprisingly well. How are the other passengers? Will they last until we get to the other side? Or do we have first cases of serious illness already? If so you know what this means? You will not be allowed to enter America and have to take this ship back. And I will have a very big problem with the shipping company after my return."

She was going to answer him but he had already turned around and marched off. She knew how serious the situation was. And suddenly she had an idea. When she saw one of the sailors she asked him if they had some disinfectant on board. He scratched his head and then smiled. Yes, he thought that they had used some horrible smelling stuff before to disinfect the cabins on a previous trip, but where would it be stored if there was any left? He would go and ask the cook. After a few minutes he returned holding a metal canister in his hand. Viktoria sighed in relief. She took it, unscrewed the rusty screw top and took a sniff. A sharp stench hit the inside of her nose. Yes! This was the right stuff! It was Carbolic acid. She recognised the smell from the hospitals in Hannover and from her father's surgery on rare occasions.

One hour later the previous stench was gone and was replaced by another. But it was – hopefully – a stench that would keep them from disease. Somebody had answered Viktoria's prayers.

Chapter 12

The days on the Concordia were always the same. The sea was calm and then the sea became rough. At the end of the twelfth day a faint coastline appeared on the starboard side. Johannes noticed it by chance as he looked through one of the portholes in the mess. He couldn't see much apart from bare red-brown rocks, no trees or bushes, no houses. Then the light went dim and soon it got too dark to see more.

After that evening's meal – again, only a few attended – he cleaned the kitchen and mess as usual. Then he went downstairs and knocked on the women's cabin door. Viktoria opened it carefully in her nightdress. "I have just seen a coastline out there. I don't know where this is but we should be in America soon now. I think it will only be a few more days until we are in New York. Oh, come to think about it, we will stop first in a town called Boston. Time enough to get some sleep now. I wish you a good night." Viktoria, having been raised from her sleep, just nodded and shut the door again.

Captain Redenius stood on the bridge and looked towards the near coast. Then he saw the light signal. He gave the order to stop the engines and drop anchor. The boats would be here in about twenty minutes. Two of the sailors went downstairs to the kitchen storeroom and brought the ominous boxes on deck. Suddenly the mysterious men were there too, watching. They looked around to see if anybody was taking notice of what was happening. But nobody was to be seen. Soon the little boats came.

Johannes, kneeling on one of the benches, watched everything carefully through the porthole. It didn´t take long for the boxes to be loaded into the boats and finally the two men followed. Soon they had disappeared into the darkness of the night. Johannes returned to the sailors' cabin hoping that nobody had missed him in the meantime. They were all asleep. Soon the engine started again and the anchor was hauled in. The freighter got up to full speed and continued its way.

Only one hour later the engines were throttled back and the ship made a sharp turn to the right to pass through a narrow entrance to a harbour. After another ten minutes the ship was docking on a harbour wall. It was very dark outside. As the ship bumped against the harbour wall everybody woke up. Commands were shouted, something was happening outside. The engine had been stopped. What did this mean?

Suddenly somebody knocked loudly at the cabin door and shouted. "Everybody out of bed, get dressed, pack your stuff. You have to leave now. We have arrived." The passengers rubbed their eyes sleepily. Then they dressed, trying to find their clothes and belongings in the dim light of the room. They were rushed onto the deck by the sailors. The captain stood at the gangway and watched them leave the ship. It took some time for all of them to appear and the captain shouted to hurry up. Johannes took a look at him. Their eyes met for an instant. Then Johannes looked out for Elisabeth´s trunk, it stood on the quayside already. No sooner had they all left the ship than the gangway was pulled up again and the ship started to move away. For a long moment they stood there in total shock.

Viktoria looked around. They were in a town with a harbour. Although it was dark she could make out other ships nearby. They must be in Boston, she thought. New York would be bigger and have more lights. Here everything was dark. Where were they? Was this America? She had meant to ask the captain but she had been hurried past him, and then he had disappeared. Before they realised what was happening the ship had gone. Now the group of passengers stood here in the middle of night, totally lost. Then they began to feel the cold. And although it was the middle of September there was frost in the air. Collars were turned up, hats were pulled over ears and shawls wrapped tighter around shoulders.

Elisabeth was the first who regained her voice. "There is something strange about it all. Where are the immigration officers? There must be something like a reception office somewhere?"

Dirtje, who stood next to her shivering with her teeth chattering, pointed at a large building in the distance. So they started towards it. Hajo Lammers and Hinnerk Frerichs took Elisabeth´s heavy trunk and followed the others.

There was absolutely nobody to be seen. Everything seemed closed. Gerti Janssen started to sob, her daughter Emmi too. A wild discussion started until

Viktoria asked for silence. "I am not sure where we are. But this is a town where there will surely be an hotel. I suggest we go up that road there and look for some accommodation. Here at the water's edge it is too cold. We do not want to catch a cold. Nor do we want to stay here all night. So, let's go!" With that she lifted her head, put her shoulders back and marched off. The others followed in a long line, last of all the men with the heavy trunk who were quietly cursing.

They chose a street going up a slight hill. Half way along they found an hotel. They had nearly walked past it but Johannes noticed the sign on the house with his eagle eyes. "Flanigan's Hotel" it read in faded letters. It was a wooden building and not very large.

Viktoria stepped up to the door and rang the bell. Nothing moved inside. She banged on the door. Nothing. But after a while a sash window was opened upstairs and a woman's head appeared. The woman stared in disbelief when she saw the group standing there in the dark. Being a business woman she quickly counted the number of heads. Fourteen! She had to get down there and open the door before they went somewhere else. A moment later she stood at the door and asked the guests to come in.

Edna Flanigan, a woman in her early sixties, turned up the lights and looked at this strange group. Where the heck had they come from? It was two o'clock in the morning, in the middle of the night! They were a sorry sight altogether. They looked tired and frozen. She quickly stepped to the open fire, stoked up the remaining bits of glowing wood and put on some more logs.

Viktoria stood in front of the group and looked at her. "Please, have you a room, many room for us? Our ship bring us here. We not know if in America. This is America, yes?" Her English was a bit bumpy because of her tiredness. But the hotelier understood.

"Well, my dear, you are on the American continent. To be precise, in North America. Even more precisely in the town of Saint Johns in Newfoundland. Where were you expecting to go?" She raised her eyebrows and looked at Viktoria. "We all book passage to Boston and New York. Now we here in middle of night and ship has gone. How far to Boston?"

Edna Flanigan stood there open mouthed. Oh, my God. What a story. "Well dear, I don't know Boston but I know that New York is very far away." She shook her head in disbelief. "I suggest I make a good cup of tea for you folks and you go and warm yourselves by the fire. In the meantime I'll get the rooms ready for you. And tomorrow is another day." With that she disappeared.

The group was thankful for the friendly welcome, the blazing fire and the very strong tea. Nearly as good as in East Frisia, they sighed. Now they relaxed and all that was needed was a bed for the night. A short while later Edna came back with her husband, Jim, who greeted the group in a very friendly manner and helped them upstairs to their rooms. Exhausted, they fell into their beds.

Outside the temperatures had dropped further and a dense sea fog crept into the harbour and took hold of the town, covering everything with a glistening icy layer.

Part 2

Newfoundland

Chapter 13

Edna Flanigan woke up to day light. She hadn´t slept well and regretted the short night. She considered to stay in her warm bed just a bit longer. Next to her snored her husband Jim. And in the next room some-body else! Oh no, the new guests! She had to go to the kitchen and prepared breakfast. Edna got up and opened the double layer curtains and took a look out-side. It was very foggy outside. Sea fog. A common sight at this time of year. The nights were frosty but during the day the sun was warming the town again. September was the gate to winter. She remembered how she and Jim had arrived here coming from Ireland to Newfoundland. It had been September too. After arrival they experienced two weeks of Autumn, then Winter from Oktober until Mai with loads of snow and ice, Spring again lasted two weeks and then Summer with high temperatures and all the wretched blackflies and moskitos. This was indeed different from Ireland. But, so she told herself, one gets used to anything.

After Edna had prepared breakfast she took a mug of tea up to Jim and woke him up. Normally it was him bringing tea to her but today everything was a bit different. She sat down on the edge of the bed and looked into the sleepy face of Jim. Married for fourty years now, she toughl. And how lucky she was having him.

"Before the guests come down for breakfast you should go and see constable Leclerc and tell him about the new arrivals. He will be interested what brought them here. It cannot be right that some ship drops them here in the middle of the night in St. Johns and then disappears again. They say that they have paid to go to Boston or New York. This is fraught to my mind." He nodded his head and finished his tea. Ian had thought about this already during the night. Soon afterwards he left the hotel and walked to the police station.

After a short but good night´s sleep the group were sitting and having breakfast. And what a breakfast it was! They was bacon and eggs, toasted white bread, yellow butter and different types of jam. But best of all was the tea. It was really strong. As they told Edna she answered proudly. "Yes my tea is strong, made in the irish tradition. My tea must have to colour of the bog water of Sligo. This is where we originally come from. Take some milk and sugar with it." The guests did.

Jim Flanigan had in the meantime reached the police station. He was out of breath as he entered the office of Leclerc who sat behind his desk having a cup of tea. Jim reported about the nightly surprise and Leclerc listend with interest. "If you ask me, Jim, there is something very strange about this. Why does a captain throw some passengers off board here in the night when their destination was America? And you said that they have paid to get there? I will have to look into this." Jim Flanigan scratched his head. Lerclerc continued. "This might be because they all got ill on the way and he knows that because of it they will not pass the immigration test. In this case he will have to take them back to Germany. Or there was some other problem on the ship, perhaps a mutiny? Who knows! But we´ll soon find out. Let´s go." He took his uniform cap and coat and they left.

The guests were still sitting at the breakfast table when Jim arrived with constable Lerclerc. They looked up in surprise. The first thing he asked was if anybody spoke English. Viktoria go up. She reported about the events of the night and this time her English was more elaborate. Lerclerc listened with interest and asked questions now and then. In the meantime a young man joined her side. He whispered something into her ears and Viktoria openend her eyes in surprise. She reported to Lerclerc what the young man had witnessed on the journey. About the stop near the ocast of Ireland and the stop last night on a coast here. In detail he described the many wooden boxes and also talked about the mysterious men who suddenly had appeared on the ship one night. Lerclerc became more and more interested and asked questions back. Here he had not only a case of illegal immigration but perhaps something much bigger! According to the description of the boxes it might even be a case rifle smuggling. And this really made him grind. Who were the two men who escorted the illegal freight?

He looked at Johannes again. "And where do you think the freighter stopped before coming to St. Johns? Was it far away?" Johannes had a good think and then pulled out his old silver pocket watch which his dad had given him as a farewell gift. " I had a look at the watch when they unloaded, it was shortly after midnight. Then we arrived about an hour or an hour-twenty in St. Johns." Leclerc nodded again. An hour north of St. Johns? There were not that many possibilities. The only harbour with enough dory boats was Pouch Cove. Perhaps he should get on this way soon and enquire further. He looked at Viktoria. "I have to asked you all to stay at the hotel until further notice. You have entered illegally into Newfoundland so I will have to inform the immigration department. And I will send the doctor her to examen you all to see if you have any contagious diseases. In any case you will be under quarantaine until further notice. Don´t leave the hotel. Sorry about this. Oh yes, I nearly forgot: I will need a complete list of all passengers with Names, home addresses, profession and addresses in the States. And don´t forget your identity papers or other relevant documents. My collegue will pick them up later on. And please tell us how much money you have for the journey. Don´t worry, it´s just for our information that we can organise something for you in case you will have to stay longer as anticipated." With those words he waved good bye and left.

Elisabeth's face became pale. The papers! They were still on the ship. She asked around. No, nobody had received the papers back from the captain. Everybody had forgotten about them when leaving so suddenly. Some couples started to argue. But it was too late. There was nothing to prove their identities.

Edna Flanigan had heard all this and it made herself think. She had a brother who was living in Pouch Cove. They arrived together coming from Ireland. Perhaps she could pay him a visit and do a bit of her own investigation work on behalf of her guests. And whilst she was clearing the breakfast table she saw the others getting more and more into a quarrel.

Viktoria tried to calm the group down. Nobody knew how long they would have to stay. How would they pay for the hotel? How much would it all cost? So Viktoria pulled Edna by the sleeve and asked .Edna couldn´t say. She had to talk to Jim first. He was in the yard. Soon after she returned smiling.

"My dears, I have just spoken with my husband. Please be assured that we will find a solution for all of you. We think to charge you one Dollar a day per person for your room and all food. And if anybody cannot pay this he doesn´t have to dispare. It is an emergency. We will find a way. This afternoon I will meet with some friendly ladies from our church knitting circle. We work for charity. And I am sure that our padre will help too. We are good catholic Christians. " With that she went back into her kitchen.

Chapter 14

Pierre Leclerc sat in his office and thought about what the young man had told him. This could turn into a very big case. Smuggling weapons into the country meant that they would be used eventually here in Newfoundland. Who would profit from that? Who would use them? In his mind he went through all the conflicts here on the island during the last ten years. There were people who wanted to get rid of the British Protectorate and demanded that they join the state of Canada instead. Furthermore there were the miners with demands of higher pay for their toil. But the strikes had been forced down. Surely, there were still miners that couldn´t keep a cool head and would be pleased to use rifles next time. He wrote down a list. Then he marched to the postal office to send a telegram to his colleagues all over the island. He hoped somebody would have heard something.

Edna was expecting the immigration officers. She answered all their questions and led them to the group in the dining room. Shortly before they arrived the doctor had left, pleased no one was showing any sign of a disease. But he demanded that nobody should leave the hotel or go into town, just in case. He looked at Edna. She gave him her promise. After all, her hotel licence was at risk and with that, her income.

Viktoria was pleased. Dirtje had recovered well and showed rosy cheeks and her appetite returned. The others of the group started to regain their former strength too. Everyone enjoyed the meals Edna

Flanigan served. But sometimes they were sceptical of the unknown dishes. The first time they were served stockfish, a speciality of the island, Edna had to explain how stockfish was made and how important this dried and salted fish was to the people here. She served fish and brewis, which was not to the liking of some as it lay heavily in their stomachs afterwards. Then there were the fried cod tongues, fish chowder, baked, stuffed squid and deep fried capelins. If you didn´t like fish in this country you had a hard time. But there were other meals that caused some discussion, for example seal flipper pie. When served that the East Frisians pushed the food around their plates. The dark and coarse-fibred meat had a strong taste so that in the end they only ate the crusty pastry. Edna, being proud of her meals, was a bit offended by this. Her guests had left the meat but took a second helping of vegetables and potatoes. When Edna one day served a dish called squirrel cake the women decided to go into the kitchen to teach Edna a few of their traditional dinners. Gerti Janssen, Sina Frerichs and Thalea Lammers took it in turns to help with the food. Edna was sceptical at first, but soon enjoyed the company and the meals of other countries. She noticed how quickly the women learned English too. She found out that East Frisians spoke Lower German at home which was close to the Dutch language and had many words which were the same in English. This made things a lot easier for all.

When the time of quarantine was over everybody went out to explore the town. St. Johns didn´t seem to be a very large place, but had several churches. One of them was most impressive. As it turned out it was the Catholic cathedral, built of pale coloured stone. They walked up and down the streets, looking at the colourful wooden houses standing in a long row. Most of them could have done with a new coat of paint, they thought, but there were brick built houses too. But the bricks were a different colour here. Elisabeth suddenly thought about the brick buildings in Emden and the wonderful Renaissance town hall near the Delft, and the visit to the advocate. How long ago had that been? Surely not more than three weeks ago? And yet, here she was, window shopping in a new and different world.

The women strolled arm in arm past the shops and admired the goods on offer in the windows. They knew they couldn't buy anything. Nobody knew what the future would bring or if they might need every penny to survive. Slowly they walked down to the harbour. Now, in broad daylight, they were finally able to see where they had landed. There were ships by the quay and the harbour seemed like a large bowl. In the distance they could see a narrow gap between large rocks and after that the open sea. On top of one rock stood a tower and on the other side an old fort, and between them was the narrow entrance to the harbour.

Elisabeth looked at her cousin. "I think we should be grateful that we landed in this place." Viktoria smiled. "Yes, you are right. They gave us a warm welcome here. They are good people and so helpful. And they like a good party. Just think of last night. All the musicians! We really did have a good dance! It was a party organised just for us! It was typical Irish music according to Edna. And our men liked the beer too. What more could we want from life?"

"Talking of the men, I think we should go and find them. Jim was going to take them down to the harbour. They should be somewhere around here." Viktoria looked around and saw Johannes standing with some fishermen. The women joined them and stared at some strange-looking cages on the ground. Inside, some large creatures of blue or dark brown colour scrambled around. One of the fishermen opened a cage and took one out and held it up towards Viktoria, rubbing his tummy and saying "Lobster, lovely lobster..." She screamed in panic and stepped back. He kept following her. Now everybody was laughing. The fisherman placed the lobster in a bucketful of sea water, then added another one. He called Johannes and gave him the bucket. "Here, my lad. Take this to the hotel and give Edna my regards. Haven´t seen the old girl in yonks. Tell 'er, I want a kiss in return." Now the other fishermen were screaming with laughter.

Johannes carried the bucket very carefully back to the hotel. He was sure that the lobsters tasted good, perhaps even better than the shrimps in Greetsiel. And if the others didn´t want any, there would be more for him. He licked his lips in anticipation.

Edna was more than surprised when she saw the lobsters. In the old days it had been an everyday meal but now the price had gone up because the upper classes wanted to eat them which didn´t leave much for ordinary folks. But two lobsters for all of them? No, she'd have to go down to the harbour and get some more. So she went off straight away and purchased another four. It took some hard bargaining and in the end an additional kiss to get a good price, but she didn´t mind because the fisherman was one of her cousins.

The very same evening the guests saw Edna covering the large table in sheets of old newspapers. Then she placed little plates on top. What was going on here? As soon as they sat down little bowls of melted butter were added and a basket of fresh brown soda bread – an Irish speciality. The next moment Jim Flanigan appeared with a heavy basket full of tools from the shed. He put a hammer, long metal skewers and a large pair of scissors on the table. The Germans looked at it all in awe. What the hell was this? Then Edna arrived from the kitchen balancing two large platters filled with the cooked lobsters which had, after cooking, turned a wonderful shade of red. She and Jim sat down and started to open the lobsters. Everybody watched transfixed. First of all the legs were pulled off, then the main body cut open with the scissors and the flesh scooped out. After that they used the hammer to break the hard shell of the legs, and a skewer to scrape the insides out. All parts were collected on one plate. Then they all went to work. It was a new and difficult challenge for all but after a while the main centre plate was filled with pieces of lobster meat and soon they could start eating. Edna poured some liquid butter onto the small plate in front of her, then dipped a piece of lobster in and put it in her mouth. The others watched and followed her example. Edna watched the faces around her. Yes, this was delicious. The bread was served too and everybody received a glass of clear water. She didn´t believe in serving beer with a meal like this, it would ruin the taste. She looked around again. The loud smacking of lips and sighing indicated that the meal was a success already.

Deeply satisfied, the East Frisians went to sleep that night. For once, the future didn´t seem so bleak after all.

Chapter 15

Pierre Leclerc sat down at his desk and sorted his papers. Being pedantic he always used the same system. To the right stood a mug of tea and a plate of sandwiches. To the left the answers to all the telegrams he had sent out a couple of days ago to colleagues along the coast. He sorted them in the right order: first of all Halifax, then St. Johns in New Brunswick, then Portland and finally, Boston in the United States. All harbours the Concordia could visit on her way to New York. He read all the documents of various port authorities and then he found what he was looking for. The Concordia had asked for permission to enter the port of Halifax to unload some freight. Leclerc looked at the dates. He was surprised that the ship had not been further south by then. But perhaps this was due to the bad weather and heavy seas of the last few days. He sent another message to the harbour master in Nova Scotia with an order to stop the ship when it arrived. Now he only had to wait for one more document, and this would come from a newspaper journalist in Halifax.

On the evening after the arrival of the stranded Germans he sat, as often nowadays, in the pub and had a beer or two. It didn´t take long until the editor of the local paper joined him. He was interested in the story of the illegal immigrants and wanted more details about the circumstances. So Leclerc told him, without giving any details of the possible smuggling. He told him about the promised destination, and that they had paid to be taken to the United States. As Leclerc spoke, the editor suddenly grabbed his sleeve.

"Hey, wait a minute! This sounds somehow familiar to me. Something like that has happened before, and if I remember rightly it happened once on the coast of Labrador and another time somewhere in Nova Scotia. And in both cases they were talking about a German ship! Now where did I hear this? No! I´ve read it. It was in the Nova Scotia Herald!"

The next morning he contacted the paper in Halifax. He did not have to wait long for the answer. Yes, it was a German freighter, but it wasn´t the Concordia, it was a ship named "Papenburg". But in both cases the name of the captain was the same – Wim Redenius! Leclerc banged his fist on the table and jumped up and down with excitement. "Now I have got you, mate." He would personally take charge in this case. He had to find out why somebody did this to his own people. And secondly, and this should have priority, he had to find out about the smuggling and if there were really rifles in the boxes. If this was the case then bloody times were ahead and he'd better take some precautions. Unfortunately, his visit to Pouch Cove hadn´t really been worthwhile. Either the people there didn´t know about this, probably a top secret operation, or they were afraid to talk about it if they did. Treason in some tight communities could prove fatal, especially when some fanatical Irish were involved.

A couple of days later he had a telegram on this desk which left him satisfied. Captain Redenius had been arrested in Halifax and the ship had been confiscated. An investigation had already been ordered. The immigration department as well as the customs and police were on board and were searching the ship. So far they had not found anything incriminating. After the investigation of the press they found witnesses in Canada and Newfoundland who swore that they had come across people in the wilderness who had been German. Most of them had disappeared and probably would never be found, others had died. There were also rumours of smuggling. A certain amount of goods were going undeclared between Europe and North America. Leclerc had already assumed this.

Around mid-morning the constable walked to Flanigan's Hotel to keep the Germans updated. He didn´t spare on the details which made the group speechless. They were ordered to stay put until the court case, and not leave St. Johns as they had to act as witnesses. This was really bad news. The Lammers, Frerichs and Janssen families had hoped to continue their journey soon. Their money would run out if they had to stay even longer. Would there be anything left by the time they arrived in Canada or America? How long until the court case? Unfortunately, Leclerc didn´t have an answer for them.

Elisabeth and Viktoria listened carefully and felt sorry for the others in the group. They understood the financial situation, although they were not directly affected. For them there was no real financial pressure – yet. Viktoria had used the time waiting to make an appointment at one of the larger Banks in town and ordered more money from Germany. They were happy to oblige. Within a month the money should be available in St. Johns. This calmed Johannes and Dirtje as they secretly saw themselves moving into a poorhouse soon. But Viktoria reassured them that she would never allow that to happen.

It was only the end of September when the first snow came. The Germans were surprised to see it. Edna Flanigan assured them that this was quite common in Newfoundland. The winters could be long and cold and she suggested it was time to buy some more winter clothes for everyone, especially decent boots.

Elisabeth and Viktoria joined the women on their shopping trip. Sina Frerichs suddenly slipped on the icy pavement and fell. She cried out in pain, she tried to get up again, only to sink back into the snow in agony. The others stood around her and tried to help her up, but to no avail. Viktoria very carefully undid the tiny buttons of Sina's ankle boot and took it off. She examined the ankle and knew in an instant that it was broken. She had seen a few broken legs and ankles in her father's surgery when she had helped him. But what was to be done now? She decided to run into the nearest shop to get help. The shop owner didn't hesitate and rushed outside. He lifted Sina up and brought the groaning woman into the shop and sat her on a chair. Then he called for one of his young assistants and sent him to get a doctor. In the meantime all the women had gathered around Sina. What a strong man, they whispered in admiration. The shop keeper instructed a second boy to make a large pot of tea. "And don't forget the sugar. Two spoons for each cup and some milk. Sugar is a must in any emergency." He smiled at Sina who immediately forgot her pain. And that she was married. What a handsome man this was.

Viktoria accompanied Sina and the doctor on the way to hospital. A coach had brought them. Now she was waiting outside in the hallway. After half an hour the doctor returned. "I am afraid she will have to stay here for a bit longer since her foot has multiple fractures. How did you know? Are you a fellow doctor?" Viktoria laughed. "Me? A doctor? No, I just helped my father in his surgery on occasions. He was a general practitioner. I would have loved to study medicine but unfortunately women are not allowed to where I come from. But I can bandage people up very well, clean up wounds and my speciality is that I'm good at holding the hands of frightened children." The doctor laughed. "Such help would be useful to me right now. You are not looking for work here by any chance?" Viktoria was taken by surprise. She'd better explain her situation. The doctor, a man somewhere in his forties, listened with interest. "Oh dear, what a story. Where will you go after the court case?"

She sighed. If only she knew. "The problem is that I am not travelling alone. There is also my cousin with her two daughters and a former maid and her brother I have to think about. We are all travelling together and are relying on each other on this adventure." She looked at him apologetically. Then she stretched out her hand towards him. "I am Viktoria Brendel from Hannover in Germany."

"And I am Doctor James Waldron from London, England. But I have been working here on Bell Island, the other side of St. Johns in Conception Bay. Not very far from here. As a matter of fact, I don't normally work here in town at all, but my best friend and colleague asked me to replace him whilst he is on his honey-moon." He was still holding Viktoria's hand. When he realised that, he let go of it in embarrassment. "How do you finance living here whilst you are waiting? You will need a job if this all takes time. So, how about join-ing me for a while and assist me on the island? Only until you know what you and your friends will do next." Viktoria promised to give it some thought.

When Viktoria returned to the hotel she found them all waiting to hear more news. She told them about Sina's diagnosis and also about the job offer she had received unexpectedly. Edna pricked up her ears. She had heard about this doctor before, she'd heard that he was working for the mining company, looking after the miners and even their families. Everybody seemed to like and respect him.

During supper that evening they asked Jim Flani-gan about this island and what kind of mines he was talking about. What did they mine? Jim was happy to explain. "Bell Island is a big rock in Conception Bay. Through this rock run layers of iron ore. First of all the mining was only on the surface, but now they are digging deeper down. The iron ore is then brought to the surface and transported to a ramp and from there it is loaded onto ships. Our iron ore is sold to iron foundries in Canada, America and even to Germany. There they make steel from it to build ships, bridges and high-rise houses. First we only had one mining company here, but now there is a second one which has permission to dig far underground and under sea level. The new tunnels will be several miles long eventually. Just imagine! Under the sea! People work down there and above them fish swim and icebergs float. I have been told that it is very cold and dark down there to work. If you ask me, it would be a horrible job and very dangerous too. I wouldn't do it for any money in the world. It is just madness."

The men finished off their beer. Most of them didn't believe this story. But Johannes had listened with some interest. "How do they transport the iron ore from down there to the ship?" Jim nodded. "Good question, young man. The miners shovel the rocks into mining cars, they run on rails and are pulled by pit ponies and horses right up to the surface. From there they are loaded onto conveyer belts driven by steam engines onto the long wooden ramp on the cliffs where the ships are waiting to take the freight."

Now Johannes got very excited. "In Germany I worked for a peat company, I learned how to lay rails and service them. I even used to drive the cars to the loading place. This would be perfect work for me. And I know all about horses. I am fed up sitting around here not being able to work. Where can I go to apply?" Jim Flanigan smiled. He liked this man. He was young, he was strong and he wanted to make money. "My boy, you are lucky. Both mine companies have an office here in town. You should go there tomorrow."

Hajo Lammers had followed the conversation quietly.

"I think this could be something for me too. I want to work as well. And when I have earned enough money our journey will continue. I'll just go and talk to my wife." He stood up and joined Thalea who was in deep conversation with Edna.

The next morning was cold and foggy again. During the night more snow had fallen. Johannes and Hajo went off to search for the first recruiting office. They found it near the harbour but were sent off again. No new workers in winter. They were advised to come and try again in the spring. Disappointed at that, they went to the second address. It was only a little way further on. It was an impressive house built of grey granite with a huge oak entrance door. Looking at that they felt very small and timid. But they were in luck, the mining company gave each of them a contract so they could start in a few days. It was arranged that Johannes would work on rails underground and Hajo above ground loading the conveyer belts. Both were going to be paid eleven cents per hour to start. They would work ten hours each day, six days a week. Sunday they had a day's rest. Work started on the fifteenth of October at eight in the morning. During the week they would stay on the island, sleeping in one of the large crew's quarters where they would also be served their free daily meals.

Overjoyed, they returned to Flanigan's Hotel and reported. Hajo's wife didn't seem happy when she heard about the crew's quarters with up to three hundred beds. She refused to go there. Edna had to laugh and took her aside. "Listen, he is going there without you.

The quarters are for men only. There is no work for women there. And besides, the miners are just as superstitious as the fishermen here, they think women bring bad luck to the island. I think it is all nonsense, they just don't want women there because they want to stay unobserved by their wives who might count the beers they drink in the evening." Then a sudden thought struck her. "But before you two start work you will have to speak to Pierre Leclerc. You will need a work permit which you only get when you have officially immigrated here. And find out if it's a problem to go to Bell Island, after all you were instructed to stay here in town. Although it isn't far away you might need a special permit."

Johannes and Hajo went off again. Edna pushed her husband to follow them. "You'd better go with them, the language is still a big problem. And you are better at arguing." Jim obeyed and followed them down the road.

Leclerc liked the idea of them going to work on Bell Island. He arranged for a provisional work permit. But he also had a special job for them. While on the island they should look out in case they see one of the mysterious men from the Concordia again. He hoped so. And if this was the case Johannes should go and see one of his contacts over there. "And please, if you meet them, do not approach them, keep away. They must not recognise you at all. They might be dangerous." Johannes promised to be careful. Leclerc gave him a piece of paper with an address and then he handed them their work permits.

Since there were some days left before they would start work they decided to celebrate the new job with a few beers and wandered off to the nearest pub.

Chapter 16

Viktoria had enlisted Edna to help her with the English lessons at the hotel. This was a hard task as a few of the Germans were hardly able to read or write. Edna could teach them many words and colloquialisms which Viktoria had not learned at her school, which were more practical for everyday conversations. If the immigrants wanted to survive they had to have a larger vocabulary. The adults found it difficult to remember all those strange words, but the children picked the new language up easily. Edna insisted that it would soon be time to send the children to school. There were Protestant and Catholic schools in town. After a talk to the parents they chose a reformed Protestant school, so the children were enrolled there.

At first the children were not happy about this but they soon enjoyed the company of other children. So there was not much time left now for them to continue their exploration of the town with its tempting shops. The girls' daily walk led past one store in particular. A sweet shop full of jars full of brightly coloured sweets which they had never seen nor tried before.

One afternoon Uda dared to tell her mum about the shop. Elisabeth smiled and got her purse out. She gave Uda two cents. Why should the girls not have a little treat she thought to herself. Uda and Feemke ran down the street. As they entered the shop the smell inside made their hearts leap. They inspected the many glass jars on the counter closely. Which sweets to buy? Oh, and there were many more jars on the shelf behind the shopkeeper. It was hard to decide. The shop-keeper smiled patiently. He knew the problem. At first visit everybody seemed overwhelmed, but soon they all found their favourite kind of sweets and would stick with them. He looked again at the girls and turned around to lift a jar from the shelf behind him and place it before the girls. The sweets looked like tiny square cushions in a lovely red colour. On the front of the jar it said "Tingling Rhubarb". He gave them one each to try. After sucking them for a while their faces lit up. Their tongues had reached the tingly bit in the middle. The shopkeeper smiled again and asked how much money they wanted to spend. Uda placed the coin on the counter. The shop keeper nodded and pointed to the rhubarb jar. Uda nodded. He took a triangular paper bag with pink stripes printed on it and the name of the shop: " O'Sullivan's – Best Sweets in Town". The bag was filled to the brim, without being put on the scales, then he handed it to Uda. Both girls said "Thank You" in a polite manner, and curtsied. Then they ran gig-gling, out of the shop. Mister O'Sullivan was happy. What lovely girls they were. So cultivated. He was sure they would come again and be customers for life. And whilst the girls walked back to Flanigan's Hotel a won-derful tingling in their mouths accompanied them on their way, bringing back memories, deeply hidden until now and released by a sweet. Memories of rhubarb in the farm garden, how they'd pulled out the sticks, bitten chunks off, how their mouths had felt funny from the acid tang. All this was there all of a sudden, making them feel nostalgic, and suddenly the vague image of a little boy crept up slowly from the deep. Enno, their little brother who they had had to leave behind.

Emmi Janssen didn´t feel like joining the younger girls. No, she considered herself a grown-up having finished school in Germany, going her own way now. So she dawdled alone through the streets of St. Johns, much to the concern of her mother who constantly warned her not go with off strangers, especially men.

One day she was watching a woman walking in front of her who had obviously been shopping with her two little girls. The woman carried two heavy baskets which she had to put down every so often. The two little girls, perhaps four years old, walked next to her, but one of them kept running very close to the road. She had never seen girls who existed in double. They looked the same and wore identical coats and hats. They had the same brown curly hair and the same faces. Only one seemed quiet and the other boisterous. The woman tried to make them stay close to her because a horse drawn carriage heavily loaded with barrels was approaching. Suddenly one girl ran right in front of the horse. Emmi heard the coachman bellow and shout, and in no time she jumped into the street, pulling the child away. The carriage passed with a shocked driver. The mother stood there, trembling, looking at Emmi who had saved the girl at the very last moment. As she came closer, Emmi could see her heavily rounded belly under her coat. After the woman had thanked her again and again, Emmi took one of the baskets and offered to carry it back to their home, then took one of the girls by the hand to keep her safe. She wasn't sure if it was the girl she had rescued. The mother walked in front of her, holding the hand of the second girl. Emmi found it very confusing. Little did she know that this encounter would change her life completely for years to come.

Gerti Janssen was happy that her daughter had unexpectedly found a job and that she was finally earning her own money. Although she was still living at the hotel she would soon be moving in with the family before the new baby arrived. She was looking forward to that. This meant a bit more time to herself. But life was not always predictable. Everybody was happy for Emmi. But her mother started to get more miserable each day. She felt more and more useless. What could she do? Apart from cooking and cleaning? She had left school at the age of twelve and then worked for six years as a maid in the household of a merchant in Emden. It had been a hard time and she was happy to have met the dock worker Jan at the age of eighteen. They got married when she found out that she was expecting a child. Emmi was their only child, and Gerti was thankful for that. When Jan started drinking they couldn't have fed another one. Jan's wages, paid out on a Saturday, had frequently evaporated on the way home, turning into beer and Schnapps. Not much was left for the family and every so often mother and child went to bed hungry. The only thing she had been thankful for was that Jan didn't beat them when he was drunk. That was quite common in many other families.

Edna Flanigan started to watch Gerti. She felt sorry for her. Gerti stood, as often before, at the window of the dining room and looked into the street. She needed something to do, someone to care for. Suddenly Edna thought of old Miss Miller who had just been released from hospital and could do with some help. Perhaps she should pay the old girl a visit and have tea with her. She liked the older woman who had been a much respected teacher here in town and she had money. Miss Miller could pay for some help. Edna liked the idea. But before she went on her visit she would have to bake some biscuits for the woman. Last time she had taken ginger ones if she remembered rightly. Or was it oat? Her memory had begun to fail her on occasions. With a deep sigh she went into the kitchen.

Jan Janssen had worked as a shipbuilder in the dockyard in Emden. He often wandered along the docks here, viewing the little shipyard. One day he dared to go closer, and to ask for work. He was lucky. The company had just received a large contract and because they could work inside a huge building the work could continue during the winter and so he was offered employment. In East Frisia he would have celebrated this at the public house, but there was no drinking for him anymore. Through the alcohol he had lost everything before; his job, his home, his self-respect and almost his wife and daughter too. He didn't want to take any more risks now that they were trying to make a new start. He was glad to have met a group a few weeks ago when he was wandering the streets of St. Johns. They had been standing on a street corner making music and praising the glory of God. He liked the dark blue uniforms they wore and the open and friendly way they talked to him. He had never heard of the Salvation Army before. Now he went to all the meetings. This gave him strength. They enabled people like him to have hope and regain dignity through prayers and long discussions. And they gave material help too. He visited the little temple in Water Street as often as possible but had not told his wife about it. Not yet, he thought, let's wait and see if it really works for me and my problems.

A mile further on Hinnerk Frerichs stood by some fishing boats and dreamed. He was a fisherman, and he missed the sea and the work out there. The boats looked different in Newfoundland. He stood and looked at the netting and noticed two men watching him. He was surprised to see anybody here at all in winter. Slowly he walked towards them. The snow was lying in dirty heaps all over town. There was icy fog every day. This weather made him restless and sad. He wished they had travelled on to America instead of staying here on this godforsaken island. And nobody could say how much longer they would have to stay. He was fed up and bored of walking the streets here. As he came closer the men looked up again and spoke, they asked him where he came from and what he was looking at here in the fishing harbour. Hinnerk introduced himself and soon they were all sitting together on the boat having tea, listening to his very strange story. Here was a fellow fisherman who needed some support and they decided to help.

In the meantime, Hinnerk's wife, Sina had left the hospital and was back at the hotel. She offered to do little sewing jobs for Edna who had complained that she could not manage all the repairs of sheets and towels since her eyesight was slowly fading. For Sina it was a good pass-time because she wasn't able to walk very well with her crutches. So she sat in the dining room mending things. After she had done all the little repairs Edna came and showed her something. It was a small colourful rug she had made years ago using a hooking needle. For this she cut fine strips of old clothing and combined the fabric with strands of wool. Sina liked the flowery motive and asked Edna to show her how it was done. But Edna shook her head at this. "I haven't got any strips of cloth left and I've run out of wool, my dear. For a rug like that you will need nice colourful wool. I will have to go to O'Leary's in Gower Street first to buy some. And we would need a second hook so that I can show you the technique." She was rummaging through a large wicker basket on the bench which contained various fabrics and she pulled out a snippet of monk's cloth. "Oh, this will never be enough for two rugs. I'll have to buy some more of that too. Perhaps two yards will do, after all it is not that expensive. I am happy to pay for it all and you can have a go at it. But not today, I am too busy. It will have to wait until tomorrow." Just at that moment Jim called for her in the yard, and off she went.

Sina had a closer look at the rug again. This looked very interesting. She turned it and looked at the back. She wanted to start right away, being generally an impatient person. So why wait until tomorrow? No way! She thought about the two dollars she had got in her purse. She could buy the things needed herself. Hinnerk didn't know about the money. Sina hobbled to the door, put her coat on and reached for her crutches. She would find the shop and if not, she could always ask somebody.

It didn't take her long to find the shop. Somehow the shop front looked vaguely familiar to her. She remembered having seen it before. As she opened the shop door a bell rang. She entered and looked around. Fabrics and yarn up to the ceiling! From the rear of the shop she heard a man calling. "Just a moment, please. I will be right with you." Sina looked around. There were fabrics of many different qualities. Thin cotton, heavy tweeds and furnishing fabrics in wonderful jacquard patterns. Respectfully she stroked the bales of textiles on the counter. Never had she seen such wonderful material before. Suddenly the owner stood right in front of her. They looked in surprise at each other. Sina nearly fainted when she realised who it was. He was the first to speak. "Well, what a surprise! How nice to see you again. How is your foot?" Sina gulped. Now the memories came back. He had been carrying her into a shop, this shop! But all she could think of were those eyes.

"I am fine. It gets better every day. And the pain is getting better now. I just hope I won't need these soon." She pointed to her crutches. Patrick O'Leary smiled at her. He had often wondered what had become of the damsel in distress. He thought of the moment he had held her in his arms and that he wished he could hold her there forever. But the broken foot had to be seen to and she disappeared off to the hospital. And now she stood right in front of him. She was a customer. "What can I do for you?" Sina stroked the jacquard cloth. "You offer a fantastic range of fabrics here. But this is not what I came here for. I need everything to make a rug with some sort of hook. And I need two yards of monk's cloth for a base. It is for Edna Flanigan at the hotel. She wants to show me how to make them. I am so bored just sitting there in the dining room not being able to do something useful." Patrick turned and got a shallow cardboard box from the shelf. "What size hook does she need? There are different sizes. Oh, have a look at this one. It's a new product from the United States. They call it a punch needle and it's supposed to be easier and faster than the traditional hook." He opened another carton and pulled the tool from the paper. It was a hollow needle with a wooden handle. " Nobody here has bought one so far to test it for me. So why don't you take it and try? Afterwards you can report back to me if it is really as useful as they promise. There is an instruction sheet with it. And if it really works you can pay me later for the punch needle. But please take two traditional hooks as well, just in case." This sounded like a good offer to her. Then she chose a colour for the monk's cloth and the colours of the wool she would need; blue, green, red, orange, white and brown. He smiled again. "Oh, here is a woman who knows what she wants. Would you like to tell me what design you are thinking of?" He looked at Sina who had started to blush. "Perhaps a flower picture. But I am not sure if I will be able to make anything at all. This will be my first attempt ever." Patrick just nodded. "I am sure it will be the most wonderful rug. When you have finished it please bring it here and show it to me. I really would love to see it. Sina blushed again. She quickly pulled her purse out and paid. With the parcel under her arm she limped out of the shop. Outside she had to take a very deep breath. That man made her mad with desire. But she was a married woman, she kept telling herself.

Chapter 17

It was a Sunday evening when an unexpected visitor appeared the moment they had finished their supper. Dr. James Waldron had come to see Viktoria. She was very surprised to see him at the hotel. They moved to the reception area and sat down. According to Edna they would be able to have a quiet conversation there.

Waldron looked at Viktoria. "Now, have you thought about my offer? Would you like to work for me?" She looked at him and nodded. "Before I decide I would like to see the place first. Where exactly will I be working? I was told that women are not very welcome on Bell Island. I find that strange, to be honest."

Waldron laughed. "Don't worry. Although I am employed by the Dominion Steel Company to look after the miners, I have my own surgery in Portugal Cove on the coast where I have patients from the surrounding area. From there is a ferry that goes to Bell Island from Portugal Cove, so when I am needed on the island I take the boat to get there. If you like, I can show you tomorrow. Then you will get a better picture of it all and you can decide." Viktoria thought this was a good idea and so they arranged to meet the very next morning at eight o'clock. Waldron would pick her up at the hotel.

Monday morning came with sunshine and a blue sky. Perfect for a day's outing. Portugal Cove was a very small village with only a few houses. The doctor's house stood out prominently. It had been built on the hillside overlooking a little harbour at Conception Bay with Bell Island in the distance. Viktoria was impressed by the fantastic view. She could see the cliffs of the island clearly and even some houses and the ferry on its way back to the coast.

James Waldron showed her the house with the surgery and his living accommodation. Then he took her upstairs. "You can stay overnight here, if you don't want to travel every day between here and St. Johns." He opened a door and showed her around. There was a bed with a colourful patchwork quilt, a small table with two chairs and a wardrobe. In one corner stood the wash set comprising a bowl and water jug, each painted with lovely roses. Above it a big round mirror with a golden frame. This all looked very inviting to her. They went downstairs to inspect the surgery rooms which turned out to be light and airy and contained all the things a surgery normally had. But looking closer she saw implements she didn't recognise. She would have to ask him about them later. They walked on. A further room contained an operating table. Viktoria was surprised. She only knew something like that from hospitals. Waldron smiled. "Yes, I have to do some operations here. Many accidents out here are severe and often there isn't time to take the patients to the hospital in St. Johns. So I try to do my best right here." He pointed to a strange looking metal ball with a pointed nose on it. "And this is the newest equipment I was given by the mining company to work with; an X-Ray apparatus. We have two of them, one here and one over on Bell Island. I am so happy that the mining company financed it. It has already saved a few lives since it was delivered here."

After they had finished the tour around the house Waldron looked out of the window. "Right, now comes the second part of the tour. The ferry has just arrived. We are sailing over to Bell Island where you will see the rest."

A short while later they were on the ferry. The sea was calm, and after thirty minutes they arrived on the island. Waldron used the time to explain to Viktoria that there were three villages on the island. "The largest place is Wabana. The name comes from the Beothuk Indians who settled here, and means 'The place where the light arrives first'. The entrances to the mines are there. At the south end of the island lies Lance Cove and west of that, Freshwater. Both are smaller villages. The first settlers here lived from fishing, hunting and some farming. The ground in the centre of the island has patches of humus which is fertile. But the largest area is covered with moors and heather. Under the surface lies the rock. And this rock is very special. In the seventeenth century it was discovered that there are layers of iron ore running through the rock. Until recently they only mined it on the surface. Later on they dug deeper into the rock. And more and more workers were needed so that the number of inhabitants increased from about a thousand to several thousand now. Many come here to work by ferry every day, but most of them stay during the week in the company-owned mess-huts. There are more than two hundred workers in each of them. This can lead to problems because of the different nationalities."

Viktoria listened with fascination. In the meantime they had walked mostly uphill and reached the first houses of Wabana where the doctor's surgery was. She saw some shops and even several small churches. Everything looked neat and tidy. Then, she saw a woman crossing the road. "There is a woman. I thought that there were no women on the island?" She stopped and looked at Waldron but he just laughed. "Oh, is that what they told you? That is nonsense. There are no women working in the mines but some men are married and have a wife and children who live here with them. They are normal families. There are new plans so that the workers here can build their own houses on the island. At the moment the mining companies own everything, but we hope that this will change soon. We will need a lot more workers here in the future and have to make it more attractive for them and their families so that they will stay. There is enough work for all."

Viktoria passed a building which was a school. Waldron explained. "There are a lot of children living here too. Most come from Irish Catholic families who have a lot of children, other miners come from Protestant England, Scotland and from Nova Scotia in Canada. So there are many religions and many chapels and schools of different denominations." He laughed, but then became sombre. "It is a great pity though, that most of the boys leave school at the age of ten or even earlier to go to work in the mines. The mine companies love to employ them because they are cheap labour. They start as Nippers who bring tea to the miners and carry messages, later they work like adults deep down in the mines. A boy gets paid 8 cents per hour, an adult, 12 cents. They should stop child labour altogether because it ruins their bodies at such an early age. They do not get very old here. But nobody dares to openly talk about it. Not because of the mine companies. No, it's the parents who wouldn't have it any other way. Every working soul is needed to make ends meet. Poverty and hunger are part of their daily life."

They finally reached the surgery which was a plain wooden building near to the mining company office. Waldron showed Viktoria around. The surgery rooms were nearly identical to the rooms in Portugal Cove. But it also had a kitchen and a woman was working in there. She had dark hair and a fairly dark complexion which astounded Viktoria for a moment. The woman looked at both of them, then continued to stir the pot of stew she was preparing for the doctor. Waldron introduced her. "This is Mabel. She cooks for me and looks after everything here when I am busy." Mabel kept stirring the stew and frowned. "I am only the cleaner here and occasionally I do some cooking." She snorted disapprovingly. What the hell had the cat brought in this time? A very fine lady. She's like a fish out of water, she thought. No good for this island. Arrgh. Perhaps the future Mrs. Waldron? She'd better be nice to her. You never know.

When it was lunchtime Mabel called them and got herself ready to leave. "Sorry, have to go, there is other work to be done at home. See you..." With that she marched out of the kitchen.

Viktoria felt most uncomfortable. "I don't think that woman likes me at all. She gave me such a strange look. Is she here every day?" Waldron smiled. "Yes, she is here every day. But she is alright. Sometimes a bit strange because she is very superstitious. But good at heart. Please, don't be frightened of her." He looked at Viktoria who seemed worried. He hoped that she would take on the job and work for him – even if Mabel was around. But he wasn't sure that Viktoria could be persuaded.

After lunch they explored more of the island. They visited the office of the mining company where he introduced her, then, they walked on to one of the mine entrances. It was a big black hole in the hillside framed with wooden logs, out of which rails ran. She followed the path of the rails with her eyes to the coast and the cliffs. Waldron stood close to her. "The mining cars come out of there and drive to the loading station. We'll pass there on our way back. Waldron led her further westwards and some time later they stood on the edge of the cliff. Waldron took hold of her sleeve and led her to the very edge. Now she could look down. The cliffs were very high. Down below was the raging sea. "Can you see the heaps of debris going into the water? Those are the rocks that had to be taken out to get at the layers of iron ore. They get dumped here. Down below us are huge openings in the cliff side. Normally at sea level to make it easier to shuffle the rocks out."

Viktoria felt dizzy. She didn't like heights and took a step backwards. Waldron had noticed and held her steady. She was thankful for that. Then they continued their walk.

Chapter 18

Edna was pleased to have a new guest who arrived at mid morning. He came from Scotland and would soon start work on Bell Island as a rock specialist. But first he had to go to see the mining company at their office in town to talk about the conditions of his contract. He needed a laboratory. Edna had not understood exactly what this was or what his job was, but it was good to have a normal guest again.

Most of the adults were out doing some kind of work. Viktoria had taken the job with Dr.Waldron. The only time they were all there was in the evenings for supper or at the weekends. Now the only ones left in the dining room now were Sina Frerichs and Elisabeth. Since the children had started school it was peaceful during the day. Sina had learned how to make rugs, the new punch needle was a blessing. The first rug had just been finished. But Sina wasn't happy at all.

"This rug doesn't look right. You can't recognise the rose. I wish I could draw better." With that she put the rug away. Elisabeth took it up and looked at it more closely.

"Well, you are right. The rose has not come out very clearly. But it could be another kind of flower. A fantasy flower. Apart from that it has turned out well to my mind. And just think, it is your very first piece. So don't be too hard on yourself." She turned the rug in her hands. "When I was a schoolgirl I could draw quite nicely. If you like I could draw the outlines onto the fabric, then you just have to follow the lines of the design." Sina liked the idea. Elisabeth started doing some drawings right away. Sina was impressed. This would solve her problem.

Edna had noticed a change in Elisabeth. Before, she had been moody and bored. But now she seemed much better, she had even gained some weight. The long and dark winter months were not for everyone, but since Elisabeth had started to draw she was much more cheerful. One day she even started to paint. She had bought some coloured paints a while before, and Jim had given her a few pieces of wood to use instead of canvas. Edna thought the paintings were excellent. There were landscapes, flowers and even a portrait of Uda, Elisabeth's eldest daughter. This woman is a real artist, Edna thought. Suddenly she had an idea. She would order some frames for the paintings from the local carpenter and hang the pictures up in the hotel. She hoped that Elisabeth agreed. After all, no one else had such wonderful pieces of art here in St. Johns. This could be good for business and bring customers.

Sina hadn't dared to go to see Patrick O'Leary to show him her rugs. But now she needed more monk's cloth, and this she could only buy at his store. So she packed three of the smaller rugs together and walked to the shop. This time without her crutches. On the way she noticed how her heart started to pulsate and a trembling went through her body. No, she thought, not again! She had reached the shop door. Just at that moment a woman came out carrying a large parcel. Sina let her pass and then entered. Patrick was just about to go into the back room when he saw her. She was even more beautiful than he remembered. He stepped towards her with a big smile on his face. "Now, what a wonderful surprise! I had given up on you. How lovely to see you again. It has been a long time. Would you do me the honour of having a cup of tea with me? I was just going to make some." Sina nodded and placed her rugs on the counter. "But before I make tea I want to have a look at what you have brought here. Can't wait to see it." He unrolled the rugs and spread them out onto the counter. He liked what he saw. Nice designs, beautiful colours and the quality of work was good. He seemed very pleased. "They are wonderful. I am delighted. You have done a great job. How was the new punch needle? Is it any good? Have you used it?" Sina felt relieved. "In the beginning it was not that easy but all of a sudden it worked for me. And it is so much faster than any hook. Even Edna said this after she tried. Now she wants one too." Sina looked into his eyes. He looked back and smiled. "Right, now I am going to make the promised tea." And with that he disappeared.

Thalea Lammers helped with some of the sewing jobs now. When Sina started on the rugs Thalea watched her but decided that this wasn't something she wanted to do. She had tried but she found it tedious. So she was pleased to carry on with the repairs, first with Sina, but now on her own. Thalea had always been good at sewing and even made some simple dresses and smocks for the women in Timmel, the place where she had lived before. The word had gotten around and soon she had had more orders than she could handle. After all, she was sewing by hand. She had told Edna about this and got an order from her straight away. Thalea had bought some blue and white fabric which she thought went well with Edna's eye colour. To make the apron special she had embroidered a red flower pattern on the top and the pockets. The fabric – called Vichy square – she had bought not long ago on special offer at O'Leary's shop. Edna was delighted with her apron and promised more orders. She would show it to the ladies from the church circle. Soon Patrick had to re-order this fabric and he decided to be adventurous and order it in many different colours. After all, wintertime was sewing time. And this year a lot of women wanted to sew.

Sometimes the wind of fortune blows the right person in at the right time. In the middle of the week a young man appeared at Flanigan's Hotel and asked for a room. He was extremely good looking, perhaps in his thirties, but maybe even younger. Edna was awestruck. He needed the room for a whole week, then afterwards he was moving on to Bonavista, so he told her. He paid in advance for his board and food. Edna's eyes gleamed. This man, who introduced himself as Jeremia Appleby, was a salesman who worked for a company named Singer from New York. He himself came from New Brunswick, Canada. There, the American company, which had produced sewing machines since 1851, had opened another factory after the first enterprise in the town of Montreal had turned out to be very successful. Now he had just arrived in St Johns by ship to 'help the women of Newfoundland to become independent through self-earned money by using his sewing machine'. His little missionary sounding lecture he ended with a loud 'Hallelujah!'. Then he grinned at Edna cheekily. Edna burst out laughing. What an amusing fellow. She called Jim who showed him to his room. Together they mounted the stairs, Jeremia in front, followed by Jim who hoisted the heavy luggage upstairs. After lunch Appleby appeared well rested and cheerful and looked for Edna again. "As I mentioned before I sell sewing machines. There is a large crate waiting for me at the harbour. It contains my demonstration machine. I was going to ask you if I could bring it here to the hotel? It would only be for a few days so that I can show the women of St. Johns what a wonderful invention it is. I want to demonstrate how easy it is to use. It will not be to your disadvantage. I will pay extra."

Edna was speechless. She had to talk to Jim about this unusual request. Edna found him out in the yard filling a basket with fire wood. He didn't object and suggested the machine could be placed in the reception area, next to the entrance. There, interested customers could inspect it without disturbing the people in the dining room. Jeremia Appleby was over the moon. He set off to fetch the crate from the harbour. Not long afterwards, a horse-drawn carriage arrived at Flanigan's Hotel and two stout delivery men unloaded the box in front of the building. They were cursing aloud because of the heavy weight. Appleby had heard this many times before and pulled out some coins for an extra tip. One of the men tried to grab it but Appleby was faster and pulled away. "Only if you bring the box inside, lads." The men complained but did as they were asked. They were just leaving when Edna came and offered them some tea and cake inside. This they could not resist. Her cakes were famous in town. Who cared about the boss? He would just have to wait.

After tea Appleby fetched a bag of tools and started to dismantle the wooden box in front of him. First he opened the top, then unscrewed the panels on each side. Soon the sewing machine stood in its full glory in reception. He looked at Edna and Jim proudly. It was a black machine with ornate gold lettering saying 'Singer'. The machine stood on a wooden top which was mounted on a beautiful cast iron stand. They walked around it and Jim gave a whistle of admiration. Appleby quickly gave it a brief dusting with one of his elbows. Edna had seen a machine like that a while ago in one of the women's magazines. Now this technical wonder stood here at her hotel. She just couldn't believe it.

Soon Appleby was on his way again. This time he took some advertising flyers and posters with him. The company had provided them, he just had to fill in the day, place and time of the work presentation by hand. Using a bucket of glue and a large brush he pasted the posters onto empty walls all over town. He handed the flyers to shop keepers and asked them to give them to their female customers. Not many refused because of the friendly way he asked. The first show would start the next morning at ten.

After finishing, the most difficult part of the mission followed. Full of confidence he walked into the newspaper office and asked for the chief editor, demanding a main article on the front page about the most modern sewing machine in Newfoundland. At the same time he would offer to place a very large paid advert on the same page. And it worked! He was pleased. Money reigned in the world. Even here, in this sleepy town in Newfoundland. After that he went for a beer to celebrate.

After supper the guests saw Appleby sitting at the machine, sewing a pair of trousers and an apron in no time at all. He had brought the ready cut out pattern pieces with him. The demonstration was a success. He had not expected otherwise. It was the same every time. When the women asked about the price he waved them off. "Ladies, enough for today. We'll talk about that tomorrow." And off he went, leaving some puzzled women behind. He went back to his room. Yes, this was his tactic. Show them the machine, work with it, and then send the women home. They would have all night, talking and dreaming about it, and come back the next day with their husbands for further sales talk. In eight out of ten cases a contract was signed the very same evening. And this contract was very special and unique so far. The sewing machine could be paid for by instalments. Hire purchase with small weekly rates. This convinced most people. And, as he told the women, this would make them independent from their husbands. Appleby wondered if the founder of the company was a Mrs. Singer. Only women knew what worked best for women.

During the coming night a lot of dreams about sewing machines drifted through the sleeping heads at Flanigan's Hotel. Such a machine would be an investment for the future. One of the dreamers was Thalea Lammers.

Only one person was not in his bed dreaming. Freerk Lammers, Thalea and Hajo's son. Hajo now worked on Bell Island, and in his father's absence Freerk had begun to live his own nocturnal life. With all the sewing going on, mother Thalea had lost track of him. He was nearly twelve years old now and decided to do this own thing. School was not for him, he didn't like the language or the way they taught. Together with another boy from school he had decided to earn some money instead. Every night he went off to work secretly. And Thalea, after having seen him go to bed in the evenings, never checked on him again. When he returned from his nightly job he went to bed and appeared in the dining room only after school had supposedly finished. He felt really bad about lying but the money he earned at the local bakery would help him to flee this wretched country. As long as nobody found out.

Pierre Leclerc paced up and down in his office, holding a telegram in this hand. He could not believe what he had just read. He went over the lines again and again. 'Prisoner Wim Redenius murdered by another prisoner in Halifax. Court case cancelled. More details soon. Signed: Police Chief Edward Baker.'

This was terrible news. The court case should have started in a month's time here in town. It had been very difficult to get permission to extradite the captain and bring him here to Newfoundland. There had been long negotiations between the Governor, who represented Newfoundland as part of the British Protectorate, and the government of Canada. Now everything had failed. What had happened in Halifax? How come he was dead? Murdered? Some strange thoughts came into his head. Perhaps somebody killed him to stop Redenius from talking. After all, if there was smuggling of weapons involved it would mean big business somewhere. And the bosses of such operations were extremely dangerous. He should ask immediately about the exact circumstances of the murder. He felt his stomach churn. And another thought came to him. Now that the court case was cancelled what should happen to the East Frisians. Could they go now and continue their journey? He had to find out right now. He took the telegram, put his coat on and went over to the immigration office.

Dirtje became more and more helpful for Edna in the hotel. She looked after the rooms, helped in the kitchen and chatted with the new guests like she had never done anything else. It was a pleasure watching the girl gaining more confidence by the day. Some guests had asked Edna if she was their daughter because Edna also had ginger hair when she was younger. This made her a little bit proud. Dirtje also loved singing and so Edna taught her some Irish folk songs and on occasions they would sing together happily. One late evening Jim and Edna sat in the kitchen and talked about the girl. Where would she go when the court case was over and everybody was free to leave? The thought of losing her made them sad. Perhaps they could make her stay? Edna and Jim were getting old, could she perhaps take over the hotel in a few years' time? Since they had no children of their own Dirtje felt like a daughter to them. Perhaps the couple should have a quiet talk to Viktoria and Elisabeth about their plans. Perhaps they could do without the girl when travelling on? At the same time Edna did not want to upset the Germans as they all felt like family now. The last few months had been the best time since they had taken over the hotel years ago. And they were proud having managed to support the group by involving various church institutions. The thought of all this and the prospect of changes made the couple sentimental.

But sooner than expected the situation would take a different turn. And it was due to Pierre Leclerc and his investigations.

Johannes and Hajo Lammers had been working for more than two weeks now on Bell Island. It was hard work there. Johannes remembered his first day when a foreman took him into the mine. Johannes could not believe that there were so many rails underground. They started walking downhill along the rails, every so often they would see a heavily loaded horse-drawn mine car coming from deep down within the mine. Johannes felt sorry for the poor horses who seemed tired but pulled on until they arrived at the re-loading place where the conveyor belt was. The further they went into the tunnel the darker it became. Soon the foreman lit a little lamp filled with seal oil and fastened it onto his cap. He did the same for Johannes. The tunnel was lit intermittently by lamps and torches. They passed some junctions and went deeper and deeper. More junctions appeared, sometimes they turned to the right, then at others to the left. How on earth could anyone find their way down here? Johannes wondered. The foreman just laughed as Johannes asked him. "Don't worry, you won't be walking here on your own in the beginning, there will always be somebody with you. Your colleagues know the way, they have cut the tunnels themselves and know every nook and cranny." Further and further they went into the rock. Then, suddenly a large stone hall appeared in front of them. This was the horses' stable. A man was just getting a horse harnessed and checking its hooves. "This is Michael, our teamster. He is responsible for all the horses down here. Without him nobody would be able to do their job. He is the most important man in the mine." He patted Michael on the shoulder. Then introduced Johannes as a new colleague. "Why don't you keep the stables outside the mine? Do they have to live here in darkness all the time?" Johannes was sad. The teamster explained that all the horses lived down here and didn't know it any other way. "Don't worry, we look after them well. One of our horses lived to the good age of twenty here. Lasted longer than most of the men." He smiled and went back to his work.

Johannes swallowed hard. What a terrible existence. Darkness and cold. Ten hours a day in dirt and sweat. Suddenly he wished himself back in East Frisia, back to the moors and his work at the peat company. There he had fresh air from the sea and the moor with all the wonderful plants and insects. And the horses there had a good life too.

Further down they walked, lower and lower. Again some heavily loaded cars passed them slowly. He had lost any sense of time and direction by now. Suddenly he heard the sound of hammers and shovels. They had reached the end of one of the tunnels. As they came closer he could make out the silhouettes of men, some cutting rocks out of the wall, others loading the cars.

"Right, here we are. This is the end of the mine tunnel. You can see a team of men here. Up at the front are the drilling men and the clobbers and here the loaders." Johannes took a closer look. But what was this? There were only a few grown men here, most of them were children. Perhaps ten years old, looking pitiful, dirty and dressed in rags. Some didn't even have an oil lamp on their caps, but they worked just like the adults. The foreman looked at Johannes's shocked face. "Well, my boy, this is life. It is normal that children go to work. Anyone who doesn't work won't have anything to eat later. Most of them are Irish. Do you realise how many of these Irish bastards have ten children or more and can't feed them? They send the kids to work as soon as they are old enough." Johannes observed two boys loading the heavy rocks into the cars. The foreman came closer. "It needs two for loading. Each shift they will have to load twenty cars. Heavy work indeed." With that he turned around and indicated Johannes should follow. He suddenly thought himself lucky to be part of the rail maintenance team.

As they scrambled further through the tunnels the foreman stopped briefly. "At this point we are actually under the sea. The sea tunnels are already about a mile long. And the ceiling above us is about one hundred yards thick. So, don't you worry. The water can't get in here." The foreman laughed. This information made Johannes feel uneasy. They walked on again. This time up-hill. After some more junctions there was a bright point of light at the end of one of the tunnels. As they came nearer Johannes realised it was daylight. They entered an area with high ceilings held by gigantic rock pillars. The whole floor was covered with debris which a few men and youths were trying to move outside. The foreman led Johannes to the large arched opening from where they could see the open sea. They climbed over the loose rocks and eventually stood on a flat plateau where they extinguished their lights and the foreman lit his pipe. Silently they stood there enjoying the fresh breeze from the sea, watching the waves breaking on the rocks before them. "Well, what do you say? Is this something for you?" The foreman looked at Johannes , gave him a friendly pat on the back. "Of course, you won't only be working down here. There is a lot of work above ground, there are new rails required and all the junctions have to be looked after. Maintenance is important and everyone's safety depends on it. If any mining cars de-rail it is

often fatal for horse and man. This must be avoided."
Johannes nodded. He was still overwhelmed by what
he had seen in the last hour.

   "Hey, let's have a little break now and something to
eat." The foreman pulled two paper packages out of
his bag and offered one to Johannes. "Here, try this.
A speciality from Cornwall – where I originally come
from. My wife is good at making Cornish pasties." Johannes opened the paper and found a longish pastry
inside. It looked golden brown with a shiny surface
and smelled delicious. "You know, the pasties were
especially made for the miners who often worked,
and therefore ate, in the dark. Have a good look. One
end is rounded, the other pointed. You bite into the
rounded bit first because it contains the savoury filling,
made from potatoes, vegetables, gravy and perhaps
meat. When you've had that you get to a kind of pastry
wall and after that you get to the jam. So, tuck in and
tell me how you like it. I am sure my wife would like to
know. She is very proud of her pasties." Johannes had
not realised how hungry he had been and in no time
it was all gone. The foreman now handed him a bottle of fruit juice. Red currant! His favourite. Johannes
felt – only for a short moment – like he was in heaven.

Hajo Lammers had, until now, not seen anything of the
inside of the mines. He worked at the ramp shovelling
iron ore rocks onto the conveyor belt which took its
load on a huge wooden construction right out to the
cliff edge and onto the ships. They were a rough but
friendly bunch from all over the world who were con-

stantly making jokes and teasing each other. There was a lot of laughter although the work was hard. Hajo didn't understand much to start with, they spoke a strange mixture of languages. But every day he understood a little bit more. And he got used to a certain rhythm in his work until he had some large blisters on his hands. The others felt sorry for him and somebody gave him some furry leather gloves to protect his hands. He was very grateful for this. As it got colder and colder another colleague brought an old pair of sealskin boots for him to keep his feet warm. He felt lucky to work alongside such a friendly crew.

Every Saturday at six pm a siren sounded from the main building which meant the weekend had started. It took a while until all the workers appeared from the mines to go back to their shacks, family homes, or the ferry. Johannes and Hajo were nearly always the first to get to the boat as they worked over ground. On this Saturday they walked to the harbour together with the foreman from Cornwall. It had already started to get dark. They found a seat on the ferry and were talking about the things they would do during the weekend. As the ferry was full they were just starting to leave as a few miners came running and shouting. So they were also taken on board and tried to find a seat somewhere. Hajo had tiredly looked at this group but he suddenly became very awake again. He prodded Johannes who was sitting next to him and whispered something into his ear. Johannes turned his head slowly and looked back to Hajo and nodded. Yes, one of the men was one of the mysterious passengers from the Concordia. There was no doubt about it. Shocked at this, the two of them pulled their caps lower over their faces and pulled their collars up. Out of the corner of their eyes they carefully watched the man. Suddenly the foreman spoke to them in a loud voice. "Hey boys, why are you so quiet? You normally can't stop chatting." Johannes whispered to him. "Have a look at the guy with the grey cap who came on board last, do you know him? No, don't look at him so obviously. I don't want him to take notice of us." The foreman waited a while and then took another surreptitious look. That face looked familiar to him. It reminded him of somebody. No, now he knew! But what was this guy doing back here on the island? And after such a long time? When did he see him last? Perhaps ten years ago? No, it must have been eight years ago. The year of the second big strike on the island. And that time the demands of the workers had been successful. They had managed to establish more rights for the workforce and founded the Wabana Workmen & Labourers Union. And it resulted in them all getting twelve cents an hour instead of ten. It was a great victory at the time and also resulted in better working conditions. But not much was left of that presently. The foreman looked again, the guy was sitting there and looked relaxed until another man joined him and they started to argue quietly. He moved his head back to Johannes. Quietly he explained. "You are right, I do know him. Haven't seen him in years, though. He used to work here as a miner around nineteen hundred and then got involved in a bad strike. In the end we got a union but they didn't want him as a member because he was a difficult and violent person. They got rid of him by telling the company that he was a danger to everybody here. So he got banned for life, never to set foot on the island again." But now he was here again. Did the bosses know? His stomach started to churn. But perhaps it was only hunger.

Chapter 19

That Saturday evening everybody had gathered in the dining room for a special weekend meal. This had become a kind of tradition at Flanigan's Hotel. Most of the women had helped Edna and Dirtje with the cooking. Now they all sat down to eat. Jeremia Appleby had already moved on, but the geologist Alec Morrison had stayed and was now part of the little party. Viktoria was fascinated to see that Elisabeth had dressed up for the evening. She wore a brand new dress of dark red taffeta. Alec and Elisabeth exchanged looks which Uda and Feemke noticed too. Their mother had been nervous and acted strangely before they came down for supper. But they were also happy to see that Elisabeth had started to laugh again and converse more easily. She had not done so for a very long time.

Only one person was missing here tonight – Hinnerk Frerichs. He had finally been asked to join a fishing crew that went out to the Atlantic to catch cod. The "Seagull III" had departed on Thursday and was expected to be back on Sunday or Monday. Sina was used to her husband's absence from her years in Greetsiel, and enjoyed being alone for a few days. This gave her some time to dream about other things. Better, to think about *someone* else. Her life had been full of secrets, secrets she should not have as a married woman. She had taken some of her rugs to Patrick's shop.

Patrick O'Leary had displayed all her rugs in the shop window and soon afterwards a cluster of women were standing on the pavement admiring them. Before he showed them to anybody he had asked the local carpenter to frame four of them. Now the first one had been sold; a rug depicting a vase of sunflowers. As soon as he'd taken the money he quickly wrote a note and sent one of his shop boys over to the hotel.

Sina nearly fainted as she peered into the envelope and saw the money and a note. In an instant she stuck it into the pocket of her apron. Nobody had noticed a thing. She would look at it later. After the meal she went up to her room and opened the envelope again. It contained two dollar notes. She blushed. For this amount of money others had to work long and hard. Then she unfolded the note. "Congratulations, dear Sina. Today we have sold the first of hopefully many, many rugs. I am so happy for you. I cannot wait to see you again. Miss you. Love, Paddy." She took a deep breath and blushed again. She must hide this letter and the money – but where? Nervously she looked around the room. Nobody must find it. Then she saw the ideal hiding place.

The meal went on for a long time. Afterwards they all sat together talking about things that had happened at work. The women listened attentively and were curious to hear news about Bell Island and the mining. Johannes and Hajo had agreed not to speak about the encounter they had had on the ferry. They didn't want anybody to worry. But it would be a good idea to contact Constable Leclerc. Perhaps he was at his office on a Sunday.

Around midnight they all went to their rooms. Edna

and Jim had gone up a bit earlier. So nobody saw Sina leaving the hotel. She had a scarf wrapped around her head, one end covering part of her face. She walked quickly to Patrick's shop in Gower Street . On the first floor there was still a light in the window. Sina knocked on the shop door. Then a second time. This time a bit louder. Upstairs a window opened and Patrick looked out. "Sina! You have come. Wait, I am coming down." Then his head disappeared." What was she doing here in the middle of the night? She must be mad. Perhaps she should turn around and go away again? Too late! The door opened with a furious ringing of the bell. She quickly checked the street, nobody there. The next she knew she had been pulled inside. Patrick locked the door again. Then he pushed the scarf down and kissed her passionately. Sina did not stop him. She had never been kissed like that before. It was the best kiss ever.

Leclerc went down into the cellar and opened the door of the police archives storage room. He was worried about what Johannes and Hajo had told him that morning. There must be something about the strikes down here. It had happened long before he had taken up his duties on the island. Perhaps there were some old files down here. With a bit of luck he would find some indication of who the trouble-makers might have been back then. He drew his fingers along the dusty shelves and stopped when he saw the files of the year nineteen hundred.

Hinnerk Frerichs was looking forward to a hot bath back at the hotel after being at sea for endless days. The fishing trip, far outside the waters of Newfoundland, had been successful. He had never seen such an abundance of fish before. The coastal fishing off East Frisia was nothing by comparison. Here they caught huge quantities of cod, herring and mackerel. He loved fishing when the catch was good. After they had returned to the harbour he was going to help with the unloading but his colleagues waved him off. No, he'd better run home to his little wife. Surely she would be waiting for him longingly. With that they winked at him. Yes, he could not wait to see her, he missed her soft, warm body.

Chapter 20

Since they had been told that the group could now officially leave Newfoundland, heated discussions were held in the dining room and in the hotel rooms. The consensus was that they would have to wait for winter to be over. It was nearly Christmas and the harbour of St. Johns had closed because of ice. There was no more shipping at all. They would have to wait until Spring. With a bit of luck this could be March or April.

But the longer their stay here lasted the more they felt at home in this country. Nearly all of the group had either found some employment or another kind of pass- time. And Edna and Jim profited as well. When had the hotel been booked up for such a long stretch? When during the winter months? Never, they had to admit.

Christmas had arrived. For the first time since arriving in this town they attended a church service in a Protestant chapel. They were surprised that one of them, Jan Janssen, was greeted heartily by many members of the congregation. Some weeks back he had told Gerti and daughter Emmi that he had joined the Salvation Army and had stopped drinking for good. They had already suspected something of the kind. Jan had changed, his personality had become more open and friendly and he seemed more at ease with himself. They had watched him praying in secret. Gerti no longer worried about him leaving the hotel and going to work, his colleagues at the shipyard were also brothers from the Salvation Army and they looked after him. Gerti had taken up the opportunity to work as a companion, looking after the retired old teacher. She enjoyed this work and was forever thankful to Edna who had arranged it. It had saved her from getting moody after Emmi had left the hotel to work for a family who now had three children. Everybody seemed to have found their place. At least for the moment.

Viktoria and Elisabeth were enjoying a few days together at the hotel. They had talked to the girls and decided to stay here in Newfoundland. Perhaps destiny had brought them to this place. Although the winters here were cold, long and unpredictable they had experienced so much kindness from everybody, and they liked the character the locals seemed to have. Their sense of humour was a bit special they had to admit. Reminiscent of the humour in East Frisia; very dry with a touch of irony.

Edna had a special treat for her guests at Christmas. By chance she had found some dainty little porcelain cups, painted with blue wind mills and strange looking figures, in a local hardware store. The shop keeper had told her that the cups came from Holland, and were given to her in exchange for something else the customer had needed. Nobody wanted to buy such tiny cups here. They ended up on a shelf in the back of the shop and she'd forgotten about them. Now Edna had discovered them and immediately thought about the tales of shallow little cups the East Frisians had used at home to serve tea. So she decided to buy the whole lot. The shopkeeper had given her a very good price. Afterwards Edna went to a store which stocked special foods and bought some strings covered with white candy rocks. They were outrageously expensive but she didn't mind since this was her present to the group of friends. Now the cups stood on the table, together with the "Kluntjes" as they were called in northern Germany and a bowl of milk. Dirtje had baked a traditional raisin loaf, the thick slices generously buttered. Edna completed this with two of her special cakes. As the door to the dining room opened everybody stood in awe, then they all cheered. They could not believe that Edna had found cups like that here. Memories came of tea times at home. Tea – the fuel that kept them going. It was part of their blood. Edna and Dirtje stood watching in the background, smiling contentedly at each other.

Two people were not happy that Christmas. Sina and Hinnerk spent most of the time in their room. Hinnerk had spent many days down at the harbour with his mates and mostly in pubs. Sina, normally very sociable, had hardly left her room to join the others. And when the couple were together they could hear them arguing. Some of the arguments sounded bad. Everyone wondered what had happened. Shortly after Christmas Edna had had enough of it and knocked on Sina's door after Hinnerk had left. She had to knock and call several times before Sina opened the door carefully. Edna looked into a face full of tears and a black eye. So she had heard right last night. "Sina, can I come in, please? We have to talk. This cannot continue. We are worried about you. What is going on?" Sina let her in and slumped down on her bed again. "I cannot stand him anymore. I don't want him to touch me. I don't want to be his wife any longer and told him so. But he ignores it all and then he insists... you know . But I can't! And if I refuse he starts to beat me. And when he is drunk he chokes me to get his way. I am so frightened!" Edna sat down beside her. Yes, she had already thought so. She took Sina's hand. " Is there somebody else?" Sina remained silent. How could she explain this to Edna, with her being such a good Catholic? Sina had never planned this. Not in a million years. It had just happened. And she had fought with herself – to no avail. She had fallen in love with Patrick at their first encounter, and she wanted him more than anything else in the world. She told Edna, who nodded. "And how does Patrick see this?" she asked quietly. Sina sighed. "I really don't know. I have not seen him for a couple of weeks. But I think he loves me too." Edna thought about it for a moment. "Well, then it's about time you go and talk to him. And if he really loves you, you come back here immediately and pack your things and move in with him. I won't tell Hinnerk where you have gone. And I won't tell the others. Better for all of us. So why wait? Move!" Sina dried her tears and put on her coat. Then she wrapped her scarf around her face and departed.

When Hinnerk returned late that night Sina had already gone. When he realised this he flew into an angry rage. But Edna stepped towards him. "Listen to me, Hinnerk. Nobody hits his wife in my hotel. And there is no raging around either. You go up to your room and by tomorrow you will be sober again. Then you will pack your belongings and leave Flanigan's Hotel, never to return. Otherwise I will call the police and you will probably go to prison for what you have done. And do not search for Sina. She is no longer here in town. You will not find her here." Jim stood next to Edna. He escorted Hinnerk upstairs to his room. "Go to sleep now, mate. And we'll talk tomorrow." Jim hoped for a quiet and peaceful night, for all of them.

Patrick O'Leary could not sleep. Sina lay in his arms. He felt her warmth and listened to her breathing. She was deeply asleep. Every so often she gave a little snoring noise. He could hardly suppress a chuckle, she sounded like the purr of the ginger kitten he had bought with the shop. This kitten had insisted on sleeping in his bed from day one. And he'd been glad of the company then. He turned his head and kissed Sina's forehead softly. She was here.

He had looked astounded when she had suddenly appeared in the shop that morning. After their first and wonderful night he had not seen her again, that had been weeks ago. She'd talked about being married which had not surprised him. He had already guessed. But that evening it was no longer relevant. And he had wished she would stay. When she left the next morning she promised to come back soon. She had to talk to her husband first. But she hadn't come. So he hoped for a visit at Christmas. But Sina still had not turned up. He had even bought a present for her. A little golden brooch with an aquamarine stone, matching the blue of her eyes. The gift was still waiting in the drawer of his desk. Tomorrow, at breakfast, he would give it to her.

On Monday morning Viktoria returned to Portugal Cove, she went to meet Waldron and together they took the ferry to Bell Island . She was looking forward to having a quiet day with him there. But she did not look forward to seeing Mabel, the house-keeper. That woman had been most unfriendly towards her and very rude. Perhaps because she had her eye on the doctor? Who knows? With him Mabel was sweet as treacle. Viktoria watched her closely. Some of the patients had told her strange things about Mabel. She had the special gift of foresight, she saw signs of nearing disaster in everything. And she believed in fairies and little green elves who gave her advice.

When Viktoria and Waldron arrived at the surgery they found Mabel sitting on a kitchen chair rocking backward and forwards, murmuring something about a disaster on the island. It was coming nearer. She became more and more agitated. Then she started praying. Waldron approached her and tried to find out what was upsetting her. But the woman seemed totally confused and beside herself. He was just trying to give her some medicine to calm her, when the door was pulled open and a mine worker stormed in. Breathlessly he reported an accident deep down in the mine. Four men were injured, and an unknown number presumed dead. They needed the doctor immediately. Waldron and Viktoria took their bags and ran. When they had reached the entrance to the mine they found three injured men on the ground. Waldron examined them briefly and gave instructions for Viktoria to take over as the injuries did not seem too severe. Then the foreman arrived and recounted how the accident had probably happened. A full mining car was on its way up and the horse suddenly collapsed. One of the passing miners disconnected the horse from the car but forgot to put the brake on the car. Suddenly the car rolled backwards down the slope, gathering speed, into the place where the crew was working, crushing them into the wall of the tunnel. Four workers had died instantly, three others were still lying down there, the rest had made it up here. Waldron ran into the mining tunnel. He was followed by two more workers with stretchers. The foreman led the way holding two torches in his hands.

Viktoria examined and bandaged two miners, helping the third one to walk back to the surgery with them. The word had got around fast that there had been an accident. As they reached the building the first women came running, offering to help. Then they saw the three injured miners and knew which team was affected. This time ill luck has passed them by. And they were grateful for it and relieved. Quietly they sent a prayer to heaven, thanking God and asking for his mercy for the others who were suffering.

Viktoria watched with surprise as the women cut the clothes of the injured, cleaned the wounds and helped to bandage heads, arms and legs. They had obviously some experience in doing that. She prepared the medication in the meantime and gave the injured the pain killers and words of comfort that they needed.

When everything was done the women left. A siren sounded from the main building. This meant that all work had to be stopped. And this at eleven in the morning. It meant that something had happened. Hajo asked the others. "Yes, it means we must stop work. There has been an accident. Hopefully nobody was killed. Look, the others are walking to the place by the office already. Let's all go now and find out. The management will inform us."

When they got there they found hundreds of men, women and children already waiting. Everybody was speculating as to what had happened and who the victims might be. Some women cried, others prayed.

In the evening Waldron told Viktoria he had not been able to save the lives of the injured. In the end there were seven miners who'd died. This affected three families. In one case a father and his two sons had perished. It was a sad day for Bell Island.

Mabel stood at the window and looked out into the darkness. She had seen it before it had happened. But it was too late to warn anybody. She wished she did not have this gift. It was a curse. And every time she suffered more pains than she could take. But it was her destiny.

There was much mourning on the island. The work stopped out of respect for the dead and their families. Work would continue after the funerals. This was a tradition of the miners, and the mining companies respected it. But the managers were not happy about it. It meant a loss of earnings, and that would not please the shareholders of the big international companies. They sat in their lovely houses, somewhere in Canada,

America or even England, counting their blood-stained money whilst drinking brandy or champagne and smoking fat cigars. That was the way things worked in the world.

But that changes had to come was the belief of a small group of men who met on the evening of the disaster in a house on the edge of Wabana. They met in secret. Their time came nearer. Soon there would be major changes. If necessary with brutal force.

Chapter 21

March had arrived and with it, higher temperatures. Ships started to move again, coming into the harbour of St. Johns. There were large ice floes on the open sea, where seals reared their young. The news got round fast and soon fishermen and seal hunters got ready for the big hunt. Hinnerk Frerichs was looking forward to being part of it for the first time. The seal hides would bring in extra income for all. On long winter evenings he had heard all about the hunt from his fishing colleagues and was eager to join them. They would start the next day just outside the harbour, below Signal Hill.

Elisabeth had started to take long daily walks, hoping to find motives for sketching along the way. She walked down to the harbour and went on towards Signal Hill – a place that held some magic for her. To her it symbolised a link between the New World and Europe. From this hill the very first radio signal between the continents had been sent in 1901. Since then the people of the two continents had become closer through radio communication. Signal Hill was also a good place to have a look at the town with its harbour basin, the old Battery and the open sea. Today she had planned to make some pencil drawings up there which she would use later for her paintings.

Elisabeth was just going to start when she discerned a larger ship in the distance, coming from the South, now heading for St. Johns. She turned her head to the North and looked at a field of small and large ice floes slowly floating past. Down below her something moved and for an instant she held her breath. On one of the floes near the beach a large white animal stood and held its nose in the air. Then it turned, sniffing again and looking directly at Elisabeth. She looked more closely. It was a polar bear, and the animal had picked up her scent. Fascinated, she took a step closer to the edge of the rock. Down below her the polar bear had dived into the water and was swimming towards the land in her direction. She suddenly realised the danger she was in. She dropped everything and ran. She ran for her life. How often the locals had told them on long winter evenings about hungry polar bears in the streets near the water and how a meeting could be fatal. She had to get away from here, back to the houses and warn the inhabitants. Near the harbour two workers were coming towards her, chatting and laughing. She shouted to them in a panic. "Watch out! Polar bear! Coming down from Signal Hill!" The men reacted immediately and ran back into town. Soon a siren sounded and the church bells were ringing. As she ran back to the hotel she saw people running in panic through the streets. Then, suddenly, she was pulled by the sleeve into a shop. Full of surprise she looked into Sina's face. Elisabeth had not realised that she had just run past Patrick O'Leary's shop. Now the women embraced each other, happy to see one an-other again. Sina looked well. Her face had filled out, her hair looked pretty and she was wearing a new dress. Not very long ago Edna had told her where Sina had vanished to. She asked Elisabeth to keep quiet about it and not to tell the others.

Elisabeth recounted her dangerous encounter below Signal Hill and Patrick congratulated her on her reaction. It was the first time in years that a polar bear had been seen that close to the town. It made him nervous since one of the shop boys was around there delivering a parcel. He only hoped the lad would know what the siren and bells meant and would search for safety. Otherwise he could be in real danger at that moment.

He looked along the street. A group of men were approaching, one of them was Jim Flanigan. They carried rifles and were obviously already on the hunt for the polar bear. Patrick opened the shop door and asked Jim to have a look out for his shop boy and order him to get to safety. Never mind where. The men strode on confidently, their eyes glowing in anticipation of a great adventure. The hunting fever had taken hold of them.

The all-clear came after more than an hour after shots had been heard. The very next day the front page of the local newspaper showed a photo of Jim and the other men with the dead polar bear. Jim stood in the centre and had placed his foot on the bear's head, his rifle hanging over his shoulder. He stood surrounded by his mates who grinned into the camera victoriously. That day every family involved bought a copy of the paper just to show their children and perhaps generations to come how brave their ancestors were on this day.

In the evening Jim celebrated his heroic actions. After a few drinks he had a great idea. He would have the polar bear stuffed and exhibited here at his hotel. Edna could not believe what she heard. She started to shout. "No way, Jim Flanigan. Not in my hotel!" Jim laughed and looked at his shocked wife. "Edna, dear, the polar bear will come. But only the fur skin and the head. We'll put him on the floor in reception. Just think of the surprise the visitors will get when they see him. And soon the word will get around and everybody will want to come and see the beast and afterwards have your tea and cake. It's good business. Just think about the big head and those vicious-looking teeth..." And with that he bared his teeth and made a growling noise. Edna ran back to the kitchen screaming and laughing. Soon she was back with a tray full of glasses. They all drank a toast to the hunters. Only Elisabeth drank secretly to the beauty of the animal. She felt more than guilty about the death of the polar bear and did not enjoy the celebrations.

Alec Morrison, the geologist, had watched Elisabeth all evening and saw the sadness in her eyes. Suddenly he was standing next to her. Without the others noticing he took her hand and squeezed it tenderly. Elisabeth let him. She looked at him and smiled. That night her bed stayed empty. Uda and Feemke had their own thoughts about it, they had begun to like this friendly and modest man and had asked themselves when Elisabeth would notice his interest in her. Now she obviously had.

Hinnerk had watched from the dory as the men hunted for the last few days. He had hauled in the hides, which were hooked in piles on a rope and then pulled into the boat. The hunters used long poles to jump from one ice-floe to the next until they reached one with a baby seal on it. They would lie there waiting for their mothers to return to feed them and made a constant howling noise which sounded like the cry of a human baby. As soon as the men had reached them they would hit them with a bat to kill them. Sometimes the animals were not quite dead when the hunters started to skin them. Hinnerk had watched this and the first time he had almost vomited, but the others had just laughed at him and carried on. The skinned corpses were left behind, sometimes writhing for a while before they finally gave up. The hunters moved on, leaving a bloody mess behind. Hinnerk promised himself he would not work like that and instead make sure that the animal was dead.

For Hinnerk the biggest challenge was the ice-floes. He could not risk making a mistake jumping from one onto the next. He thought about his life in East Frisia and how he had jumped the widest ditches using a long pile called "Polstock". He had won many competitions in his time.

The next morning he joined the others again and drove out to sea with the dory full of hunters. They worked in teams, two of them rowing and hauling in the hides, the others hunting. Full of excitement they left the harbour and rowed out to sea. They did not have to search for long before they spotted the first baby seals. Now the hunters started the slaughter. Every skin would bring money so they worked as fast as they could. Today Hinnerk would be joining in the hunting. He jumped off the boat, then onto another floe, and continued until he reached the one with the young seal. The animal looked at him with large dark eyes and made a crying noise. It had never seen a human and didn't know that there was imminent danger. Hinnerk choked, he took out the heavy club from his belt but hesitated for a second. Had he been looking sideways at that moment he would have seen the danger. Just at this instant the mother seal had returned and slid back onto the floe, ready to defend her offspring aggressively. With her weight the floe started to tilt unexpectedly and Hinnerk slid towards the edge, still trying to grip the long pole which he had been sticking into the ice. But he could not prevent himself from sliding. The mother seal mounted the floe and attacked him. Hinnerk tried to fend her off but to no avail. Then his injured body slipped into the icy waters right next to the furious seal.

The other hunters did not see this happen, they were some distance away. Only one of the rowers had watched the attack and immediately alerted the others, pointing to the ice-floe where only shortly before Hinnerk had stood. The seal and its baby had gone. There was blood everywhere. They searched the waters but they could not find Hinnerk. Soon they realised that they had come too late. Nobody would survive more than three minutes in the icy cold of the sea.

Early in the afternoon Constable Leclerc came into Patrick's shop and asked for Sina. Patrick told him she was upstairs, working on another rug. Patrick looked into the sad eyes of the policeman and asked why he wanted to see her. Leclerc gave him a brief report . Patrick was shocked. He calmed himself for a moment and then called Sina. When she came down the stairs she looked into their serious faces. "What's the matter? Why is the constable here? Have I done something wrong?" Leclerc didn't know how to explain. Then he straightened up and took a deep breath." I am sorry. I have to make a sad announcement. This morning your husband had a fatal accident. He went out with others to hunt seal and slipped off an ice-floe and drowned. The men could not help him in time. Afterwards they searched for him and only after an hour they found his dead body. They have brought him ashore and now he is in the hospital to be examined. Before he drowned he was attacked by a seal. You will get the death certificate tomorrow. I am very sorry to bring bad news."

Sina stood there stiffly. Her eyes wide open in disbelief. Then she started to scream. Patrick stepped towards her and took her into his arms. He felt her swaying, Leclerc pulled out a chair, and both men carefully helped her to sit down. Nobody said a word. Then Sina collapsed in tears.

Chapter 22

April had nearly ended, having been unusually warm and mild. In the middle of the previous week Edna had received a letter from her youngest brother in Pouch Cove. It was an invitation for the coming weekend. His youngest son was going to be christened. The invitation was for both of them which made her gasp with surprise. Edna smiled. Finally! It had taken two whole years for her brother to forgive Jim. All the trouble because of a stupid remark that Jim had made. At the time Edna's brother had built a new kind of boat, a design not known until then. It did not look like a traditional dory. And Jim had ridiculed the boat builder, had called the boat an ugly thing and said that it would sink on the first trip because of its shape. Brian was deeply hurt. He had built the boat using some improved techniques and had been proud to present it to his friends and family . Jim had regretted what he had said ever since. After all, the boat was still floating and in daily use. It had not sunk, as Edna kept telling him every so often. Now the conflict seemed to have died a quiet death. And about time too.

  In the evening Edna told Viktoria and Elisabeth about the fishing village north of St. Johns. She suddenly had an idea. "Come to think of it, you could come too, take the girls out of town and have a little picnic on the beach whilst I am in church. The weather looks good so far. How about it? Elisabeth wasn't sure if she felt like an outing. A picnic on the beach? Sand in her boots and on the sandwiches? Edna smiled. She knew

Elisabeth by now and continued to try to convince her. "Just a little day out for the girls. And who knows! Perhaps you will see one of the many icebergs drifting past. Now, you would not want to miss this?" The prospect of an iceberg convinced Elisabeth and Viktoria hugged her cousin joyfully.

So, on Sunday morning, the group went on their way to Pouch Cove. After an hour's travel by horse-drawn coach they reached Brian's house. The family greeted Edna and Jim, then the others. The family went off to the church. Viktoria , Elisabeth and the girls were shown the path down to the beach which led off from just behind Brian's home. They carried a blanket and two heavy baskets with treats for the picnic that Edna had prepared the evening before. The path led over a stretch of land with rough grass, low bushes and heather. In Newfoundland they called it Tuckermore. Soon they reached the edge, looking down onto a grey-brown sandy beach surrounded by rocks of all sizes and shapes. Carefully they climbed down over the rocks, looking for a sheltered place as the wind was still icy. Then they unfolded the blanket and opened the baskets. But Uda and Feemke had already left, impatiently running towards the water's edge.

Uda saw it first. Then Feemke. Everywhere little dead fish. Some were still moving but looked as if they were dying too. And with every wave more were rolling in. There must have been hundreds, if not thousands! Uda yelled for the adults to come and look. She was almost hysterical. So the grown-ups came running. Speechless, they stared at the fish before them.

Elisabeth panicked. "Let´s get away from here quickly. We don't know why they are dying. Perhaps the water is poisonous, perhaps the whole beach is dangerous!" She pulled the girls back to the rocks. Viktoria remained calm. "I am going up to the house to find out what this means and if it is safe to have the picnic here. You just stay put and don't panic. I will be back soon." With that she clambered up the rocks again and ran back to the house. Having arrived there she knocked on the door. Weren't they all in church? No, she could hear voices from inside. And then the door was opened by an old lady, probably the grandmother. She looked at Viktoria suspiciously, who, out of breath by now, tried to explain about the many dead fish on the beach. The reaction of the old woman startled her. She saw a look of surprise and then a big toothless smile. Grandmother turned and shouted something into the house and all of a sudden some children came running out, shouting "Caplin are 'ere, Caplin rolling". They ran up the street and two dashed to the nearby church. Grandmother told Viktoria to go back to the beach. Soon there would be people coming. Nothing to worry about.

At the church the christening service was just about to finish when the door was pulled open with a bang and Brian's eldest son ran in and shouted "Caplin are rolling!". Everybody looked at each other in disbelief. At this time of the year? Then everybody got up and the whole congregation ran back home. Brian kissed his baby son on the forehead and off he went, closely followed by the padre who quickly unbuttoned his surplice only to throw it onto the last pew before he ran after the others. Edna looked at her sister-in-law, they both began to laugh. "Well now, what a surprise. Caplin! They could not have chosen a better day! It's only April! The world has gone mad, indeed." Then the two women ran back to the house. The baby in his mother's arms was bobbing up and down and obviously enjoying this unexpected pleasure.

When they reached their homes, people exchanged their Sunday best for work clothes. Then everybody rushed outside, grabbing any buckets available and ran bare footed, down to the beach.

Elisabeth had spread out the blankets and unpacked the baskets for the picnic in the meantime. She watched Viktoria returning, talking to the girls down by shore. Then, all of a sudden, people came from every direction, holding buckets and shouting. Fascinated she watched how the women turned up their skirts, tying them to the waist and exposing their legs. And off they went into the water, scooping up the fishes, handing the full buckets to their children or men who ran back to the house to empty them there and return.

Viktoria and Elisabeth enjoyed the jolly atmosphere until Elisabeth suddenly shrieked. She saw Uda and Feemke alongside Jim, standing in the water too. They had done the same as the women, showing their naked legs and even their knickers to the world. Elisabeth nearly fainted. Her girls in the middle of dead fish! Their clothes ruined by the smell and salt water. Where was their good education? It was so embarrassing! Then Edna arrived back from the house, carrying a huge cast iron frying pan. Her face gleamed. "What a wonderful day! Normally the Caplin are rolling much later in the year."

Viktoria wanted to know more. Why did the fish die here and in such great numbers? Where was the fish being brought to and why? Could one eat them? Edna was happy to explain. "The Caplin are a real blessing for us here. We fry and smoke them or keep them salted in barrels for the winter. The leftover fish we use as fertilizer for our gardens." Elisabeth turned away in disgust. She could just imagine the stink. It reminded her of the gardens in Greetsiel where the fishermen used to fertilize their gardens with the shells of the shrimps. Horrible!

Edna explained further. "You can also make fish oil or fish meal from it. But you can also preserve them by salting and drying them on the wooden stakes. You have surely seen them here along the coast, I mean the wooden constructions near the harbours. Our winters are long. You need full stores here in the out ports. There are not many shops here where you can go and just buy something you might have run out of. It's not like in St. Johns, where you have a shop on every corner." This seemed logical to Viktoria. But why were the Caplin dying here – on this beach? "They come here to spawn near the beach, the males add their juice and after that they all die here. The fertilized fish eggs are washed deep into the sand by the waves where they are protected from being eaten by predators. And one day a load of little fish appear from the wet sands and swim out to sea. And when they are grown up and ready to spawn they will return to the beach they originally came from. This is the circle of nature." At that she clapped her hands. "And now, ladies, we all go and collect some dry wood on the tuckermore for a fire here on the beach. We will have fried Caplin for lunch today." She pointed at the frying pan. Viktoria and the girls followed her enthusiastically. Only Elisabeth followed grumbling all the way.

Chapter 23

When Doctor Waldron went to collect Viktoria on Monday morning, he saw that she was very excited. She told him all about yesterday's trip to Pouch Cove and the rolling Caplins. He had never heard of this before and listened closely all the way to Portugal Cove. Waldron had to look at her every so often as she was talking so enthusiastically, her cheeks gleaming. She was so full of good humour. He had never seen her like that. What happened to the cool, reserved and professional woman he worked with? He knew her age, but right now there was a young woman sitting next to him sparkling with joy over her experience. Never had she been more beautiful. A new and strange feeling came over him. For a moment it confused him. But then he realised what it was. He was falling in love with this beautiful and intelligent woman.

The whole day they worked side by side at the surgery in Portugal Cove. The work was the same as ever but there was a strange tension in the air. Viktoria noticed that her boss was even more distant than usual, and after the last patient had gone, she followed Waldron into his office and shut the door. He sat behind his desk, hardly daring to look at her. "James, what is the matter today? This morning you seemed so relaxed when we were driving here. But since then you have treated me with such distance. What have I done to you? Did I make a mistake?" She looked directly into his eyes. He looked down onto the desk top. Then he got up and stood right in front of her. Their eyes met. "Viktoria, I don't know how to say this. I think it might be wrong to say anything at all." He looked away again, this time inspecting the tip of his brown leather shoes. They were covered in dust, he thought, they needed cleaning. He would do that tonight. Viktoria was confused. "What are you trying to tell me? What is wrong?" He didn't react. She took him by the shoulders and shook him in frustration. "Talk to me! Please!" Now he saw panic in her eyes. James Waldron took a deep breath. "Viktoria, I am sorry. This morning, on the way here, it suddenly occurred to me that I have fallen in love with you. I know this is highly unprofessional. But I had to tell you. There is no other way. What do I do now?" He looked like a little boy who has been caught doing something outrageous. Suddenly, Viktoria burst into a hysterical giggle. Then she whispered into his ear."Well, for a start you could kiss me. Let's see where we take it from there..." For a moment he thought he had not heard her properly. Then he realised what she had said.

That evening Viktoria did not return to St. Johns.

The next morning they took the first ferry over to Bell Island. Mabel was surprised to find them both already in the kitchen drinking tea. Waldron and Viktoria looked so happy. She looked into their faces and knew. Quickly she murmured an excuse for disturbing them. As she left the kitchen, Viktoria and James heard her say something like "...about time too...better late than never". In the hallway a metal bucket was put on the stone floor with a bang and then Mabel started to scrub the floor tiles ferociously.

Mabel had seen it from the beginning. The very first time Viktoria had entered the kitchen she knew that this woman had come to stay. She gave a little sniffle and then smiled. This would be a good reason for a decent meal today. Our Doctor being hooked like a cod needs some celebration.

Chapter 24

It was the middle of May and Spring had arrived in the East of Newfoundland. The gardens were full of daffodils and primulas. Bell Island showed itself off with an abundance of wild flowers. The days were full of sunshine and warmth and an air of optimism swept the island like a light breeze.

Viktoria used her free moments to stroll over to Lance Cove and its harbour. Or sometimes she visited the village of Freshwater. She enjoyed discovering more of the island and on the way back often walked across the nearly overgrown paths in the middle of the island, where, one day, she even discovered a small lake. Since coming to work for Waldron she had been surprised how large Bell Island really was. In the office of the surgery she had found a map on the wall which she studied, often with a cup of tea in her hand, during a break. She tried to memorise the locations of the different mines, the fastest routes to get there by, and where exactly the entrance of each place was. This could be important in an emergency. She discovered the drawn in paths across the plateau and areas of moors and tuckermore. But nowhere could she find a marking of the secret gardens that Mabel had talked about on many occasions. How could she find them?

On her walks across the island she rarely met anybody else. Occasionally she noticed a woman in the distance, vanishing so fast that she began to think it had been an illusion. Then one day a woman carrying a heavy basket and garden tools was walking further ahead. She decided to follow her, perhaps to one of the gardens, out of curiosity.

The plateau of the island was covered with moorland. In many of the shallow hollows black peat had grown, in others fertile soil had gathered. Those hollows were used by the locals of the three settlements as gardens, the rich soil and the sheltered site made it possible to grow vegetables earlier than anywhere else on the island. Some of them even had root cellars, built into the shallow dips, the front being a stone wall with a door, the top covered with sods of turf. Some gardens were surrounded by a low wall to keep animals out.

Viktoria was still following the woman. After a couple of miles she went down to a garden and called out to somebody. She put the basket down and then the tools. She called again and gave a whistle. Viktoria quickly dropped down onto the grass. She didn't want to be seen. Then, all of a sudden the door of the root cellar opened and a man scrambled out and got to his feet. The moment he got up she realised who it was and felt immediately sick. It was one of the men from the Concordia. The woman unpacked the food and they both sat down on a flat rock to eat. She could not hear what they said. But she did not dare to go closer. In fact, she thought, she should turn around and get away immediately. So she crawled backwards very quietly only to find that her skirt was in the way. She stopped and listened, but nobody seemed to have noticed her. After a while she got back up on her feet but did not dare to stand upright. When she had reached the narrow path again she walked as fast as she could towards Wabana. She looked down at herself, her dress had been torn and her arms and legs were scratched from the bushes and the rough grass. But she had to rush on. When she reached the loading area where Hajo was working, she felt relieved. Seeing him, Viktoria waved and called to him. He looked up in surprise, had a quick word with his foreman and walked over to her. Still shocked, she told him about her close encounter. Hajo listened with great concern. As soon as he finished work he would pass on this information. Hajo tried to remember who Leclerc's contact on the island was. He just had to find the piece of paper again with the name and address. But where was the paper? It was months ago that he'd received it. He just could not remember.

After returning to his shack in the evening he searched. Finally he found the paper in one of the inner pockets of a winter jacket. He read the name and went on his way.

It was a mild and moonlit night. Only a slight wind moved the grass and leaves on the plateau. In one of the gardens four men sat, discussing the final plans for the coming event. They had argued for weeks amongst themselves whether to take over the mines and if so, when? The members of the miners' union were opposed to the plans. They found the ideas of the two outsiders too radical. They themselves only wanted better working conditions. They had no understanding of some of these radical changes and it was of no interest to them to start a revolution inspired by some communists or socialists. All those ideas – thought up by some foreigners far away. What did they know about Bell Island? Nothing! And to use rifles to enforce their demands was out of the question for the two union members. But tonight they were here. Now they had lost their influence they at least wanted to know about the timing schedule of it all. There should be no nasty surprises for the workers nor for their families when the trouble started.

Just as the union men got up and were going to leave, there was a sudden sound of crackling in the bracken all around and footsteps were heard. Then, a loud voice. "This is Constable Leclerc! Put your hands up! Don't do anything stupid, you are surrounded. We are coming down now. You are all under arrest!" The two union men put their hands up in the air and waited. The other two pulled out pistols and started to shoot at the edge of the dip in the direction of the voice. The police immediately returned fire. Quickly the union men had dropped to the ground and out of the firing line. They saw the others fall. The very next moment the police swarmed in and secured the pistols of the revolutionaries. Behind them stood Dr.Waldron and Viktoria. She had led them to the right garden thanks to her good sense of orientation. Both of them came and examined the injured, bringing the emergency bag for first aid. Luckily there were no fatalities.

Leclerc was satisfied. His colleagues were good marksmen. But there was still something in the back of his mind. He asked for a torch, went to the door of the root cellar and opened it very carefully. Here, somebody had made themselves comfortable. And moving closer he found what he had been looking for. The long wooden boxes had been used to make the base of a bed. He called his men and they opened the lid of one box. Yes, inside were brand new rifles. The same night the revolutionaries were taken to the prison in St. Johns.

In the coming days more men were arrested as well as two women. After this the local newspaper published a brief article about the operation. Although the editor had questioned Leclerc as to how he had known where to find the criminals, he did not give any details. He felt an obligation to protect his informants. After all, this would only be the beginning. Somewhere out there were others, trying to overthrow law and order in Newfoundland. But he would not rest until the last of them was behind bars too. Some things just needed time and good research. But he mentioned none of this to the editor.

A few weeks later, sometime in June, Leclerc received a thick letter from Halifax. He looked at the envelope with trepidation. After he had read the contents he was devastated. He paced up and down in his office, then made a decision. He sent a note to Edna, asking her to set up a meeting of all of the Germans at the hotel the next evening at eight. He had to inform them of something most important.

The next evening everyone sat in the dining room, curious as to what Leclerc wanted. Everybody had come, only one was missing – Hinnerk Frerichs. The constable had arrived on time and looked earnestly into the faces before him.

"Thank you for coming. The reason for our meeting today is a letter I received only yesterday, which came from Halifax. To be precise – two letters. The first one is from a Mister Caldwell, who works as a reporter for the largest newspaper in Halifax. Here we go:"

"Dear Mr. Leclerc, Please find enclosed a letter written by the prisoner Albertus Meiners, who has been held at the prison of Halifax for more than a year now. He was sentenced originally for theft and disturbing the peace on more than one occasion. I heard about him and visited him in prison where he told me his story which deeply shocked me and reminded me of something I had read a while ago in a copy of a paper in St. Johns, Newfoundland. I started to research further and came across your name in the case. Perhaps you can help me. Please read the enclosed statement. There is a copy of the original version in German and for your reference I was able to obtain a translation into English. I will need your support and the support of the Germans who were dropped in St. Johns and hope they are still there. Expecting a positive answer I remain, yours faithfully, Ian Caldwell."

He looked up into the startled faces in the dining room. He handed the translation to Edna and Jim. Then he gave the original German statement to Viktoria. She cleared her throat and started reading it aloud:

"My name is Albertus Meiners, I come from Muenkeboe in East Frisia, Germany, a poor community in the moors. About a year ago my wife and I decided to emigrate to America, taking our little son, who was at that time just one year old. In Emden we took a ship with the name "Papenburg" together with another family from Eilsum, Krummhoern. We had a terrible crossing. One day we had supposedly reached our destination. The captain, one Wim Redenius, made us disembark in the middle of the night on the coast, but not before his sailors had robbed us of everything we had like money and papers. When we protested they beat us up. The ship departed very quickly and left us in an uninhabited and wild land. Many days later we were found by some native hunters. Unfortunately their help came too late for my wife and son. They died of hunger and cold. The same goes for the other family. Only we men were strong enough to survive the ordeal. What haunts me is that we could not bury our loved ones in the rocky ground, we had to leave them to the wild animals. With the help of the hunters we managed to eventually get to Halifax and reported our ordeal to the police. They sent us away, they did not believe our story. Instead, after a few days they had me arrested for theft and begging. I could not show any papers to them and explained that they had been stolen. Nobody believed me. The prison here is not a good place. Nobody should be kept in such conditions.

One day a new prisoner was brought into my cell. It was Wim Redenius. He did not recognise me because I had a long beard and long hair by then. At first he ignored me and kept muttering to himself. But when he realised that I might understand him, he talked about himself. And all the while he did not know who was facing him. At one time he bragged about all the stupid East Frisians he had taken on his ship wanting a better life in America. And he told me how he had dumped them somewhere along the way in the wilderness, and that he had robbed them of all their belongings. He laughed at that hysterically. And he was proud of having destroyed all evidence of their existence by burning their papers and the passenger lists so that nobody could blame him for their disappearance. He also talked about the extra income his smuggling had provided and how much money he had earned from that over the years. At that moment I could not bear to listen to him anymore and so I jumped up and grabbed him to stop him. I just wanted to shut him up. I pulled him up by the collar and strangled him until he was silent. As I did that I kept on calling "You have murdered my wife and son, you bastard." By the time the prison warder had unlocked the cell Redenius was already dead. I have to admit I don't feel sorry for killing him. Now I am sitting alone in my cell waiting for the trial. They want to see me hang. But now this journalist has come and promised to help me. I am not very hopeful that he can, but perhaps there are other people out there who have also suffered the same fate. How could he be so cruel to do this to his own people? To destroy the lives of innocent passengers in such a terrible way? We probably will never know. All that is left for me now is to lay my life in God's hands. Signed Albertus Meiners."

Viktoria put the letter down. It was very quiet in the room. Everyone stared at Leclerc. Viktoria was the first to speak. "This is so terrible. Now we know that Redenius had done this to others too." She looked at the group. "We are blessed that he brought us here into this harbour and did not dump us somewhere out in the wilderness. Oh, I can't bear to think about this." Elisabeth agreed. "Oh my God, the poor man! And they will hang him now? This cannot be true! We have to do something!"

Then havoc broke out. Everybody was talking, shouting and some were crying.

Jim used his loud voice to bring order. Then he gave the chair back to Leclerc who tried to calm them. "Yes, my dear friends. I agree. We have to do something and we have to do it fast. That is why I sent an urgent telegram to the courts there yesterday and received an answer by return. Because of that I have allowed myself to book a passage on a ship this morning for all of us to go to Halifax. The Canadians have officially invited us to be witnesses in the trial. We can only hope that it will help Meiners' case to come to a good conclusion. And even if he has to stay in prison for a while I will make sure that he can come here afterwards. I think St. Johns is not a bad place for stranded souls. Am I right?"

At that moment Edna arrived with a tray of drinks. She had not forgotten to bring a glass of water for Jan Jannsen. He gave her a grateful smile. Then everybody lifted their glasses and said "Cheers". Johannes got up and shouted. "To a fair trial and to a good outcome. And to our new home here in Newfoundland and to new friends!" Then they all knocked their drinks back.

After that they stood looking down at the ground. They were still shocked and would be so for a long time. But somehow life would go on. Nobody knew what the future would bring. Life was just like that.

THE END

Postface

Whilst working on the script of this book I was asked how I found the story of this novel and why it is set in Newfoundland. Well, as often in life, it was by pure chance.

As in many families in East Frisia – I come from this part of Germany – there have been ancestors who emigrated to America. In my flat stands a little writing cabinet, dating back to 1908, which was given to my great-grand mother by her brother, along with a black and white photograph. It shows a man, aged perhaps around thirty, with a huge beard and incredibly piercing eyes. He emigrated that year and took a ship from Bremerhaven to New York, later joining other Germans in the state of Iowa.

Because of this I had always had an interest in the subject and was more than delighted when the "Auswanderer Museum" in Bremerhaven opened in 2005. I have been a frequent visitor there ever since. Fascinated by the many documented stories I also heard about other tales, fraught tales of, deceit and disaster. Enough inspiration for a story, I thought. And that my novel is set in Newfoundland is really some kind of destiny thanks to three women. Two of them I cannot name because I never asked their identities. But a big "Thank you" should you by any chance come across this book. First of all there was a young woman, deeply engrossed in a book as I was trying to buy a ticket for an exhibition at the National Museum of Canada in Toronto. When she finally noticed me she apologised. She was just reading an interesting book by Annie Proulx, the story set in Newfoundland, and her ancestors came from there. Now she wanted to visit that place, having been made curious. She was so enthusiastic about it that after the museum visit I went straight into the nearest book shop to buy a copy.

A few months later, being long back home, I happened to see a little advert in a glossy magazine celebrating country life. The bold heading said "Newfoundland in winter. Take a holiday of a different kind" with an email address. This caught my attention and I sent a message and asked for more details. The answer came from Dr. Elke Dettmer, a German woman, who had been living there for twenty years in a small fishing village on the East Coast. There she had a little guest house. She was more than surprised to get my enquiry. As we found out later a German friend had placed the advert unknown to her as a thank you for a great holiday she'd had at Elke's home. The next weeks some messages were going to and fro and in the end I booked a holiday with her. She was not only a wonderful host but also a very competent guide. She drove me around the Avalon peninsular, showing me nature, historical sites and introduced me to her local friends. Some more holidays followed. On one of my visits we took the ferry to Bell Island. It was unforgettable. We explored the remains of the mining industry in Wabana, streets where once upon a time life had pulsated, now often reduced to foundations of former shops and homes. But there were still people living there, houses with huge murals showing scenes of the once all important mining history. It was impressive but at the same time depressing. Eventually we reached a little cemetery and I wandered around trying to read the names on the headstones, faded and overgrown with moss and algae. The names could have been from grave stones in England, Scotland, Wales or even Italy. And then I stopped. There was a name which you probably could find in East Frisia today. At this moment the idea for this story took its beginning.

As soon as I returned home I started to write. I used the research material I had gathered in Newfoundland, found out that the on Bell Island the mined iron ore had been exported to America, Canada, England and even to Germany. Ships from Emden transported the freight to be later shipped to the large industrial areas along the river Ruhr. I found out that on occasions the captains of freighters took passengers over to America. But when they were taken ill on board they were illegally dropped somewhere on the way. That way the ship's owners did not have to pay for the return trip.

After the first five Chapters had been written I unfortunately had to postpone my writing. Life demanded other things of me. For twenty years the fragments slumbered somewhere in my computer, eventually the files were copied from one gadget to the next and I nearly forgot about them. Until the Covid- lockdown ended all my activities and gave me time to look for the Chapters again. I found them but could no longer open them. A good friend of mine helped to restore them. So, a big thanks to Andreas. What would I have done without you? And when I finally read the Chapters again the memories came back too. At last the story has now been finished. And this after twenty years. Some projects just take their time.

Christel Weingart, September 2020